A Light in Space

by Wendy Orr
illustrations by Ruth Ohi

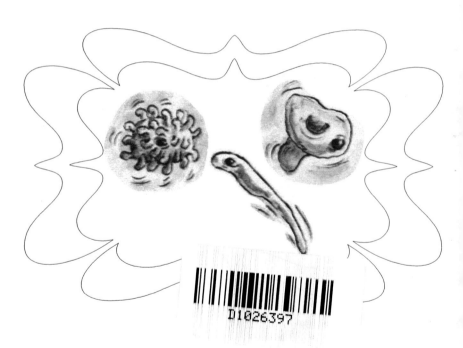

Annick Press
Toronto • New York

The editor wishes to thank Istvan S. Szabo, and the staff of the
Ontario Science Centre, for their assistance.

Annick Press Ltd.

Annick Press gratefully acknowledges the support of the Canada
Council and the Ontario Arts Council.

Canadian Cataloguing in Publication Data

Orr, Wendy
    A light in space
(Annick young novels)
ISBN 1-55037-368-4 (bound) ISBN 1-55037-975-5 (pbk.)

I. Ohi, Ruth. II. Title. III. Series.

PS8579.R72L5 1994   jC813'54   C94-930968-0
PZ7.O77Li 1994

Distributed in Canada by:
Firefly Books Ltd.
250 Sparks Ave.
Willowdale, ON M2H 2S4

Published in the U.S.A. by Annick Press (U.S.) Ltd.
Distributed in the U.S.A. by:
Firefly Books (U.S.) Inc.
P.O. Box 1338
Ellicott Station
Buffalo, NY 14205

Printed and bound in Canada by Quebecor.

To my parents,
who taught me to believe in the individual.

Chapter One

Ysdran slowly circled the dark mass. A mysterious, heaving surface, unsafe to land on, its rolling ridges made her afraid to even hover too closely above it.

But there were lights at its borders. Lights!

Curiosity fought with fear, and won. She pointed and Starquest JE6479 (The Bucket, Ysdran and Caneesh called it) flew a fraction lower.

'I knew it!' she exclaimed. The lighted area was on solid ground – but that still didn't mean it was safe to land. Not when her main instrument panel had just so spectacularly blown up. Luckily, the tiller and speed controls were separate.

She could go a *little* closer. She didn't need to land; she could hover just above the surface.

Her thoughts flicked towards Caneesh.

'There are no planets left to discover,' he

announced. *'Therefore, there are no rules for undiscovered planets.'*

She would have to make up her own mind.

The movement of the dark mass still made her nervous. She might even have turned around but for those flickering lights. A whole colony of lights, some moving, some still. They almost reminded her of a city – except that it was impossible.

She cruised lower and lower. The solid ground was higher than the treacherous dark area – and suddenly she was there, skimming above the surface of an unknown planet. She flicked the switch to Hover.

No lights directly below; they began a short way farther in. The surface was definitely solid, but uneven.

That was when she saw it – something moving.

She was too excited to be afraid. She came in closer.

A monstrous, primitive kind of life form, huge and upright. It was lumbering slowly forward on two thick antennae, with a pair of thinner feelers dangling from just below the head.

'It's hideous!' Caneesh exclaimed. *'Horribly hideous! It's the ugliest thing I've ever seen!'*

'It must be injured – look at the way its feelers are drooping.'

'Hideously horrible!' Caneesh repeated. 'I'm not looking at it again!'

'Or it could be very young; maybe it's not quite finished.'

'Not quite! You were more finished than that when you were hatched!'

'There's another one!' Black against the dark ground, and so much smaller that Ysdran hadn't noticed it at first, the second creature was still longer than her ship. Four stubby antennae let it cruise along the surface, circling the taller monster. 'That's a much better specimen.'

'I don't know about "better,"' Caneesh objected. 'Maybe not quite as horrible.'

A primitive communication cord ran from the smaller creature's neck to the dangling feeler of the other.

'I was right! The big one is not fully formed. The black one's controlling it.'

The small monster, sniffing along the ground, suddenly touched something with his nose. Jaws opened, a tongue flashed, and the thing was gone before they could even see what it had been.

'What a fabulous future!' Caneesh sniffed. 'Being trained by a mobile black hole.'

Ysdran ignored him. This was amazing. Incredible! She had not only discovered a whole new solar system – she'd discovered a planet with a

7

completely unknown life form! She was going to be extremely, incredibly famous, the most famous Junior Explorer in history.

The larger creature looked up. Looked up and straight at her.

Ysdran felt the shock. Felt their minds meet.

'What are you?' she heard. *'You can't be real!'*

'Of course I'm real!' she snapped. *'Are you alive?'*

'Of course I'm alive!'

Then, both minds together, *'I can't believe this is happening!'*

Without warning the mind link snapped.

The two creatures began to move, at about ten times their previous speeds, towards the lighted area. The bigger one stayed upright, but its dangling feelers were pumping furiously, obviously not injured at all.

Ysdran was suddenly terrified. She was within the reach of giant unknown aliens, and far out of reach of civilization and help. Maybe it was time to be sensible rather than brave – and the only sensible thing to do was to get right out of this solar system. She pointed to ESCAPE, and the little ship shot upwards.

She had seen the planet from a long way off. A planet where no planet should be, in a solar system where no solar system should be – according to the charts of the InterGalactic Mineral Exploration

Company. And they were the best maps in the Universe.

'*Remember Rule One Thousand and Three,*' Caneesh had reminded her. '*"The Company is never wrong."*' Yet Ysdran had discovered a new solar system.

She'd circled five of its planets on her way towards its central sun; as she'd approached the sixth, her Mineral Monitors had begun to bleep madly. "Hydrogen!" they screeched. "Oxygen!"

She'd flipped the switch to Cruise, and cut her speed back until it was safe to reduce altitude. Slower and slower, lower and lower, until the Mineral Monitors were going so fast and so loud that the bleeps became one long, drawn-out scream.

That was when the instrument panel had blown up. A shriek, a bang, a flash of blue light, and bits of control board – everything but the speed controls and tiller – were scattered all around the cabin.

Had she gone Space Crazy? Instrument panels didn't blow up. Instrument panels were solid, safe and indestructible: instrument panels were what their lives depended on.

Even Caneesh had been shocked – another thing that was supposed to be impossible! A Companion's job was to keep the Explorer calm and happy when life went crazy. He wasn't supposed to go crazy, too.

'*Oh, Space Junk!*' she'd sworn. '*I'm in a solar system that doesn't exist, without instruments and with a Companion in shock; I might as well find out all I can about this place!*'

'*Find out how?*' Caneesh demanded. '*With no instruments? Flying* blind!'

'*The old-fashioned way.*'

'*But you don't have old-fashioned senses! You're a modern, superior being –*'

'*I know, I know.*' – But she'd gone on anyway. And her eye had been good enough to spot the aliens...

Now, as she climbed steadily out of the strange planet's atmosphere, she was still wondering if she should have stayed longer – and even whether she should go back and try to spot the creatures again.

A cloud of dismay filled the ship.

'*You don't think it's a good idea? To get a sample of the hydrogen and oxygen – and maybe a specimen of the aliens...?*'

'"*No alien life forms allowed in space craft,*"' Caneesh reminded her. '*Anyway, they wouldn't fit.*'

'*There must be smaller ones!*'

'*What you really mean is, "Thank the Great Explorer for rules."*'

'*True,*' Ysdran admitted. Now that her excitement was dying, she didn't know if she would dare to return. The chances of landing and exiting safely, without instruments, on an unknown, unthinkable planet must be a million to one.

'Three million,' Caneesh flashed, 'and our chances of getting home –'

'Don't tell me.'

'If I could run like this in Track and Field,' Andrew thought, 'I'd clean up in the Olympics by the time I was thirteen.' It was funny how that thought came into his head, popped in as if part of his brain didn't know that he was scared out of his mind and running for his life...

He didn't even look to see if it was following him. He couldn't stop to think whether a twelve-year-old boy and a small black dog would be able to outrun a – a what?

A UFO. An alien spacecraft. A flying saucer.

His street at last. Johnsons' house – Komijaks' – Franklins' – his. He threw himself in the front door, sobbing for breath.

"Andrew? How many times have I told you not to use that door with Max?"

He couldn't say anything. He leaned against the door, still panting, blocking anything that might try to come in. Max flattened himself against his legs, quivering and whining.

"Andrew?" His mother's voice was high and sharp with sudden anxiety. "Is that you?"

He tried to answer, still couldn't speak, and heard her quick call: "Bob! There's someone at the front door!"

Andrew's father was not tall, but solid. Strong. He had strong square hands and a square jaw. He was as wide at the waist as he was at the shoulders, and he looked as if nothing on earth could knock him over. Even alien spacemen would not want to tackle him.

"Just a funny-looking boy with a funny-looking dog!" Then he looked at Andrew's face and stopped teasing. "What's the matter?"

"I – I saw a spaceship."

"No jokes. What happened?"

"I did; a flying saucer – not a saucer – more like a miniature torpedo..."

"Look at that dog!" his mother interrupted. "He's scared out of his wits!"

"Since when did that dog have wits?"

"Very funny! Come here, Max!"

Max slunk over to her, ears flat against his skull, eyes popping. He whimpered as she picked him up, and hid his head under her arm.

Andrew knew how he felt.

"A spaceship came in over the sea," he insisted. "We were in the park above the beach, and it came down low, hovering above us – I could have nearly touched it. I could see the pilot."

"If there was a pilot, it had to be some kind of aircraft."

"It wasn't a person, Mom! It was –"

"A little green man?"

But what Andrew had seen was weirder than any little green man. All he knew was that it was alive, and it had spoken to him – "speak" wasn't the right word, but he couldn't exactly say that they'd beamed thoughts straight into each other's heads.

Heads was wrong, too. It didn't have one.

"More like a jellyfish – with two tentacles. It asked me if I was alive."

Her first trip! Ysdran gloated. The most junior Explorer of the InterGalactic Mineral Exploration Company had just discovered more hydrogen and oxygen than anyone had ever recorded. On her very first trip! It was unbelievable!

She suddenly wondered whether it was so unbelievable that nobody would believe her. Unless the record had been saved when the instrument panel exploded. It might have shot out just in time.

No such luck. Bits of dials, meters and gauges drifted vaguely across the cabin – but no records.

13

Not one. Nothing to say where she'd been or what she'd found. No sensors to tell her where she was going or what she was going to meet on her way.

It was almost too awful to think about.

Caneesh's thin mind rubbed hers. *'We still have the charts – and my enormous knowledge. We'll get home.'*

'You forgot my skill.'

'No, I didn't. But I still think we'll get home.'

Home. Images of Rougita floated through the air: the beauty of mines and factories lit by the pale red sun; the perfect formation of a soldier-tribe gliding through the streets; Ysdran's cell in the Junior Explorer Block, with space for Caneesh and a Data Bank, and – if you hovered in exactly the right place between the ceiling and the end wall – a view of the Chief Explorer's Palace.

Thinking of the Chief Explorer brought her back to reality and the question of whether her story would be believed. It was too bad that Caneesh couldn't tell anyone else what they'd seen. But if Caneesh had been able to communicate with anyone but Ysdran, he wouldn't have been on Starquest, *'So I wouldn't have seen anything anyway!'* he reminded her.

Eons ago, when the InterGalactic Mineral Exploration Company was founded, the young Explorers had been allowed to take along any pet they liked. The Explorers were happy; the Company was happy, because happy Explorers didn't go crazy; everything was fine. That is, until the century when a Deputy-Chief Explorer decided to interview all the Companions when they returned, to check on exactly what the Explorers had been thinking while they were away.

The result was – Space Madness. The worst outbreak in history. Junior Explorers collapsed under the strain of trying to think only nice thoughts about the InterGalactic Mineral Exploration Company – and especially about the Deputy-Chief Explorer. Pets became unable to rub minds, refused to talk – in fact, stopped being Companions – all from the fear of an interview with the Deputy-Chief Explorer.

Finally, the Chief Explorer had her own interview with the Deputy.

Old Rougitans say pieces of that meeting can still be seen as small orbiting moons in the Twelfth Galaxy.

True or not, from then on, Caneesh's tribe had been bred specifically to be Companions, and they were now the only ones allowed on long voyages with their Explorers.

Ysdran had been given Caneesh on the day she hatched. For a century they had lain side by side in the Explorer Nursery – two fat, formless blobs –

and then, slowly, gradually, they had begun to shrink. When they were small enough, they returned to their own tribes to begin their training: Ysdran learned to fly, while Caneesh's memory was filled with Company rules, useful facts, and statistical probabilities.

Ysdran shrank a little as she remembered the loneliness of the crowded training barracks – the endless rows of students, hovering competitively, jealously guarding their thoughts, all striving for the same prize: to graduate as a Junior Explorer. She'd never asked what happened to the unsuc-cessful candidates; she was just relieved to know that she was on the path of power, with her own spacecraft, her own cell – and Caneesh back again. For the first time since she'd left the nursery, she didn't have to guard her mind. Their thoughts were shared as soon as conceived – but Caneesh could not share them with anyone else.

It made him a perfect Companion. No matter where in the universe they were, she was his whole world.

'That's not what makes me perfect – it's my wonderful wit, my breathtaking brilliance and startling statistics!'

'Rules and regulations!' Ysdran scoffed, but it was true: Caneesh's intelligence was more sophisticated than anything else in the universe

(except, of course, for Explorers). He must be eons more advanced than the monsters they'd just seen... *'Those creatures are so primitive it's amazing they're alive!'*

Andrew woke up after ten o'clock. His mother had sat with him for most of the night, as if he were still very young and having a nightmare. He'd tried to explain that he wasn't so much afraid as excited.

"This is amazing!" he kept saying. "A real, live alien – and I saw it!"

"Yes, dear," she kept repeating, still as if he were having a nightmare.

His father had left the room at the first mention of alien jellyfish. He shouldn't have said jellyfish, but it had been the closest thing he could think of: about the same size, and made out of... jelly. The shape was different, though. There'd been tentacles pointing to controls, but they weren't solid, seeming to just flow out from the body. A body the colour of sunrise: pinky-yellow and glowing. He wasn't sure about the head. The more he thought about it, the more it seemed as if the whole body was head.

And it could communicate. It thought the same way he did. It was real and alive and resented being

17

asked if it were. And it had been scared and excited, too. He didn't know how he knew that; he just knew.

Andrew wasn't bad at drawing, and sometimes it helped him sort things out. Now, he set paper and pencils carefully out, as if this were some sort of test. These drawings, he thought, would go to whatever the UFO branch of the Armed Forces was called – and probably be circulated around the world! So he had to get them right.

The first few weren't even close, but as he drew he started to see more clearly what the alien had really looked like. Its body wasn't solid, he was sure of that – it changed shape depending on what it was doing. He drew the way it was when they'd looked at each other and "talked."

He remembered more as he went on. There had been something else in the ship, something like a mechanical mouse, sitting upright.

The spaceship itself was easier. He'd had much longer to look at it, from the time he first saw it as a pin-dot of orange light coming in over the sea till it had hovered just above his head...

What if he'd been brave enough to leap up and grab it? He had a feeling that he might not be here if he had. If there really was no life anywhere in the solar system except on Earth, this little alien had come from a long, long way away: blob or not, it had more advanced technology than he could possibly imagine.

Maybe it had even stranger powers. Sketching in the spaceship's outline, Andrew suddenly realized where the orange light had come from. The ship was transparent, and had no lights at all: it had been the glow of the alien itself that he'd seen from so many kilometres away.

Anyone who tried to grab and catch that would probably end up fried or in several million pieces! Andrew was glad that he wasn't particularly brave.

He couldn't get the back of the ship quite right – it was something like a torpedo, but the end was like nothing he'd seen in any space or aircraft book. He started a new sketch just as his mother came in.

"This is what I was talking about."

"I was hoping you'd be back on earth this morning!"

Andrew smiled back, but it would never have made a toothpaste commercial. If your own parents didn't believe you, who would?

She sat and put her arm around him. "You had a bad scare last night, I can see that. But tiny flying saucers with English-speaking jellyfish? Come on! Tell me what you really saw."

"That is what I really saw!"

"All right, Luke Skywalker; just tell me when

you're ready." She left the room quietly, shutting the door behind her.

Andrew turned back to his drawing; something was still not quite right about the little alien.

Suddenly a picture flashed into his mind and he sketched in three fine antennae. Perfect!

But why three? Yesterday, he thought, it had two. Now he could see it clearly – as if it had sent a new picture into his brain!

The shock made him drop his pencil. It rolled to the edge of his desk, he grabbed at it, missed.

He always was a lousy catch. Missing a rolling pencil was not weird.

What happened next *was*.

The pencil stopped in mid-air and rolled gently back to him – all the way to the pointer finger of his right hand.

"Did you see that?" Andrew yelled, as if anyone could have. "The pencil came to me!"

He heard something like a laugh, coming from inside his own head.

'Wasn't that what you wanted?'

"Who said that?"

Andrew spun around, expecting to see a tiny spaceship.

Nothing. Max looked up casually from chewing a stick to see whether the game was worth joining.

So Max wasn't scared. And if Max wasn't

scared, the alien wasn't there... But it could still talk to him.

Caneesh scoffed: *'That communication cord from feeler to neck seemed a little limiting!'*

'It might make life simpler: at least they wouldn't have to worry about whether it was their Thinking Day.' The skies around Rougita were so jammed with thought waves that Junior Explorers were only allowed to think on every second day. (Lower classes were allowed to think once a year, on their holiday.) Even so, accidents happened: Ysdran remembered the night a simple order to a guard had jammed and she'd ended up discussing the meaning of life with an elderly Explorer. She hated things like that. She had too much to do in life to worry about the meaning of it.

There were more serious problems, too. Spaceship landings had to be done entirely by instrument, since no guiding thoughts could ever penetrate the communication fog. That especially was something Ysdran did not want to think about.

The monsters' planet had plenty of problems in its atmosphere, a shocking imbalance of gases, but no communication fog. No thought waves.

Ysdran remembered the shock when her mind

21

had touched the alien's. This was another living, thinking, feeling creature. It was the most amazing thing that had ever happened to her. Primitive, weird, monstrous as it was, the alien had responded in the same way that she had.

Now it had happened again. Touching an alien's mind once was a fluke; twice was a pattern – something that could go on happening. With no interfering thought waves between here and Rougita, the possibilities were endless!

'What about the smaller one?' Caneesh interrupted.

'I couldn't communicate with it at all. Its mind was filled with an image of itself digging a hole in the ground. I couldn't get past that.' Caneesh sniffed. He wasn't jealous, but he didn't think it was healthy for Ysdran to spend so much time thinking about these aliens. *'What else is there to think about up here?'*

'How to get us home, for a start!'

'You mean, think what we've got to tell when we get there! A whole new solar system, a planet that's an absolute storehouse of minerals...'

'If you can figure out how to get them.'

'And a species of aliens unknown to science!'

'Mountainous monsters!'

'They could be trained,' Ysdran insisted. *'I'll bet you –'*

'What?'

'A month's holiday on the moon of Uturk.'

'Okay,' Caneesh agreed. 'A month there would be just right after this. No extraordinary explosions, no blind blundering, no crazy creatures. Because there's no way that you can teach that alien any useful powers before we get home.'

'I can, and I will. I'm going to present the Company with a perfect treasure trove.'

Chapter Two

One shout, Andrew thought bitterly, and his bedroom was overflowing with parents, looming like inquisitors.

His dad was gazing around uncomfortably for something to study, and chose the drawing of the spacecraft. "That's nice. Interested in rockets, are you?"

Andrew stared at him. He sounded like a visiting teacher, making conversation with a kid he'd never seen before. "Hey, Dad!" he wanted to say. "Remember me? Your son, who's wanted to be a pilot since forever?"

"Not as much as airplanes," he muttered.

"Who were you talking to just now? More intergalactic blobs?"

"No one." His dad shrugged; his mother gave him her I'll-get-to-the-bottom-of-this look. "I dropped a pencil and it rolled back to me."

"Really?" his mother said brightly. "The slopes in this house do some funny things, don't they? I think the builder had a few problems."

"Which reminds me, I hear there's been a bit of a problem with drugs at your school. Anyone offered you anything?"

"Oh, great, Dad! I see something weird, I tell the truth, and automatically I'm on drugs! Thanks a lot!"

Andrew slammed out of his room and out of the house. Great Saturday. Usually he went over to Kerry's, but now he didn't want to see anyone. He walked fast, head down and hands in his pockets, but his dad, puffing along like an out-of-condition whale, had caught up to him by the time he reached Franklins'.

"Thought I might need a walk, too."

The Franklins' Rottweiler answered for Andrew, smashing itself furiously against the fence, teeth bared, and giving a reasonable impression of what it would like to say to them. John Franklin, a bony, bald-skulled man, looked smugly up from polishing his car.

"He thinks a big dog makes him a big man," Andrew's dad whispered. "Next time he should buy a whippet."

In spite of himself, Andrew laughed.

"Maybe we should have a look at where you saw the spaceship."

"You believe me?"

His dad shrugged. "It's a crazy world. I don't know what I believe."

They ambled around the park, skirting the Saturday morning balls and kids, trying to look casual. "A spaceship should leave a burn mark on the ground – something like that," his dad said. Andrew was sure that the glowing alien hadn't scorched the earth, but he was hoping he'd be wrong.

He was right.

"I don't know what you saw, Andy. A spaceship would have to leave some kind of sign. It could have been a hoax."

Pretty elaborate hoax, Andrew thought, but he wasn't ready to talk about the second incident – he still wasn't quite sure himself what had happened. They wandered a bit further.

"I didn't really think you were on drugs! But you hear so much about it these days – I had to ask."

"Mm."

"Well – that's about all the morning exercise I can handle! You coming home?"

"In a bit."

Skirting the path to the beach, Andrew cut across the park and scrambled down a rocky cliff to his favourite spot. It was in a hollow behind a scrubby, low-hanging tree; once you'd scuttled in, you could huddle there forever without being noticed, gazing out over blue water and green islands. Sometimes whales passed, sleekly magnificent in size and majesty, but today there was nothing in the straits but the white-capped waves and a distant fishing boat.

He'd never brought anyone here with him. If he found litter he always decided that it had blown in from the park above. This was his own private thinking place. Nobody else's. And right now he needed to think.

Maybe the story did sound weird, but it was true. And he wasn't the only one who'd seen it; it had scared Max out of his tiny dachshund mind. Wasn't that some sort of proof?

And then the pencil. That wasn't anything to do with the slope of the house. Things normally fell *off* his desk. They never leaped back on.

Would it work again? He wasn't sure whether he wanted it to.

He shut his eyes and pointed. If there was something there when he opened them, he'd try the pencil trick again.

There was: a round, white stone by his left foot; right where he was pointing. He flicked it away, and then willed it back as hard as he could.

The stone skipped down the cliff and out of sight.

Andrew swore.

He hadn't wanted these powers, but now that

they didn't work he was angry. More than angry – desperate.

That pencil had moved; he knew it had. He hadn't gone crazy and he hadn't made it up. It was terrifyingly weird and he didn't want anyone to see it, but he did want to do it just once more, to prove that it was true. He tried till his face was red and his hands clammy – with sticks, leaves, and rocks... He couldn't call any of them.

The answer struck him all of a sudden, when he'd already given up and was clambering back up to the park. He hadn't done it – the alien had. It was the shock of seeing the alien in his mind that had made him drop the pencil in the first place, and afterwards it had laughed. "Wasn't that what you wanted?" it had said. Somehow there in his mind, somehow working through him, the space creature had moved the pencil.

Figuring it out didn't make him feel any better.

The little ship zipped through the strange planet's atmosphere on Hyperspeed. With nothing but Ysdran's own weak eye to guide her, that speed would have been crazy in traffic, but from what she'd seen of this planet there wasn't going to be anything to hit.

One thing did flash by, white, with a trail of cloud behind it. Ysdran was out of range before she could see more, but it didn't look like a meteor or comet.

'Some sort of spacecraft, maybe?' She cut her speed back a little.

'Built by those creatures?'

'It would have to be very simple.'

'It would have to be very large,' Caneesh corrected, doing some quick calculations. *'But it's impossible. A ship big enough to carry that monster couldn't possibly fly.'*

Ysdran laughed. *'Add it to our list of discoveries, Caneesh: a new kind of asteroid, found only in this solar system.'*

She pointed her speed back to Hyper.

Kerry's house was six blocks away, but might as well have been in another city: a city where everyone lived the way they wanted, without worrying about being the same as everyone else. There were no square-box little houses with square-box little gardens, all lined up in a row, the way they were on Andrew's street. The houses here were scattered and private, back from the road, with high fences or hedges; all different and all huge. The Miltons'

30

house, with its surprising angles and glass, was probably the oddest and biggest of all.

And needed to be, Andrew thought, as he rode his bike up the driveway to the sounds of Chris' violin, Robin's trumpet and Randal's cello.

Kerry was lying on his stomach in the family room, playing video games. He waved a foot hello and went on shooting. Andrew wandered into the living room to look at the aquarium.

It filled the end wall. The tiny, brilliantly-coloured fish – electric blue, black-spotted yellow, silver and gold – flicked through graceful fronds of seaweed and nosed in miniature caves. Andrew loved them. They were part of the magic of the Miltons' home, an unexpected island of peace in the bustle.

But today their magic didn't work. The longer he stared at a tiny yellow fish, the more it changed into that other, strange, yellow creature he'd met. And he'd never noticed before that those little silvery fish were shaped exactly like torpedoes... *Think about something else.*

"Have you started that essay yet?"

"On freedom of speech? We've still got another week..." Kerry said. "Have you noticed that adults only believe in freedom of speech for themselves? Freedom to say what we think in class, that would be worth writing about." He groaned. "Want to play? I just died."

31

It was a relief to stop looking at the fish. Andrew took over the joystick. He wasn't as good as Kerry, who played nearly every day and often made it right to the end to destroy the alien planet's missile base. This time he got shot down before he'd even left Earth's atmosphere. He groaned and rolled over.

"Let's go up to your room."

There was a sudden bang, and a smell like barbecued sneakers. The boys gagged as Mrs. Milton came up the basement stairs to open all the windows and doors. "Don't worry," she muttered distractedly, and went back down again.

"A new spell she's working on," Kerry said. "I don't think that's exactly the effect she's searching for."

"Doesn't smell like it." So things didn't always go right even for Mrs. Milton! Andrew didn't believe in magic, not really; he knew there were tricks to it. Just like he knew that Mrs. Milton was Kerry's mother – as well as Chris', Randal's, Robin's, Jamie's, Alex's, and Sam's – and that she cooked and gardened and checked homework just like ordinary mothers. But when he watched her show, part of him still believed that she was a real magician, doing real magic. And so he couldn't help believing that things must usually go the way she wanted.

"How's Max?" asked Kerry. Max was the only thing Andrew had that Kerry didn't (four of his brothers and sisters were allergic to animals; Mrs. Milton was one magician who never pulled a rabbit out of a hat).

"Okay. Sort of. He was pretty scared Friday night." – And it all rushed out. "We saw a UFO, Kerry! It came right down to us, a little tiny one!"

"Oh, that," Kerry said airily. "Hovered over our house for a while."

"You're kidding! I saw it coming in from the sea; I wonder how long it was here?"

"There could have been more than one. What did yours look like?"

"Silvery; transparent." Andrew sketched it in the air. "The – the pilot was orange."

"Mine was bigger and gold, and the pilot was red."

"Have you told anyone?"

Kerry's eyes lit up. "They swore me to secrecy."

"Who?"

"The aliens. Last time they came they beamed me up to their space ship for a demo flight. They were going to zoom me back to their planet – pretty neat, eh? – but at the last minute I told them to take me home. They might come for me in a few years, they said, when they need a new leader."

Andrew felt like he'd been punched in the stomach. For a few seconds he'd thought Kerry was serious.

He should have realized. This was Kerry in full story-making flow. His round, freckled face had begun to glow; the glazed stare was in his blue eyes. Andrew had seen that look before, and he knew there wasn't much point in trying to tell Kerry anything now.

"Come on," he said, "let's find a football, I need to kick something."

Kerry, broken off in mid-story, stared at him. Something was eating Andrew today. He *never* wanted to play football. Basketball, soccer, baseball, hockey... never football.

But they'd been friends since kindergarten. Sometimes you just had to put up with it when your friends went weird. "Okay," he agreed. "We just have to watch out for Jamie. She's trying to rake up the leaves."

Ysdran loved it. She was flying with nothing but her own senses, the way the pioneers had, eons and eons ago – and she was farther from home than any Rougitan had ever been. She was a true adventurer.

'Do you think my senses will grow?' she asked Caneesh. *'I might end up like some prehistoric creature, the way I'm learning to use my eye!'*

'I don't think we'll live long enough.'

35

Ysdran ignored that, and studied the map. *'We'll come in here, in line with the three southern stars of the Paradise Galaxy.'*

'I don't know why you had to go off the chart in the first place!'

'How do you think anything was ever discovered? An Explorer's job is to explore – to find our minerals – new wealth, new planets!'

'And,' added Caneesh, *'you turned the wrong way.'*

'That, too.' She hadn't meant to. If she hadn't been daydreaming when the needle showed that it was time to turn... if she hadn't panicked when she finally woke up, and pointed left instead of right...

'We'd be home now – instead of this wild wandering while you find our way!'

'I'll find it! Besides, a chart is only something that tells us where Explorers have been before.' Time to change the subject. *'Isn't it wonderful out here? I've always been so busy looking at the instruments that I've never had time to notice anything else!'*

Caneesh screamed.

A huge, dirty-grey ball was hurtling towards them: a comet, so far from a sun that it had lost its glowing tail. It filled the front windscreen.

And the right windscreen.

Ysdran pointed to the left Jump button, and Starquest bounced fast and high, and barely a squeak out of the comet's path.

It slid by to their right, so close that Ysdran felt she could have pointed out the window and touched it; so close that she could have studied its surface if she'd been calm enough; so close that if one speck had been thrown off...

A sudden horrible memory struck her. *'Didn't we go through a ring of comets to get into this solar system?'*

'A catastrophic comet cloud,' Caneesh agreed. *'I didn't enter the exact number, but between sixteen and seventeen trillion.'*

'Funny: they didn't seem to matter so much when they were just blips on a screen.' Ysdran pointed her speed down to Cruise, as slow as it would go. That way she might have time to see what was coming before she crashed into it. *'I wouldn't mind a few instruments now,'* she admitted.

'So you do want to return to Rougita! You've changed your mind about dying in a daydream?'

Ysdran swivelled her eye. There were two small comets on the left, and a larger one to the right. That left several trillion that she couldn't see. It was going to be a long flight.

The two small comets slid past, were replaced by three more. Her eye was already aching with the strain.

'A long flight,' Caneesh repeated, *'and you might have to keep your mind on the flying instead of your*

new friend! Which reminds me: how soon could we book into the moon of Uturk?'

Ysdran waited as the bigger comet whooshed by their right window, scanned the sky again and pointed her tiller slightly to the left before she answered. 'Not for a long time, since I'm going to win the bet, and you'll take me to the Ghost Planet Belmor.'

'Why in space would you want to go there?'

'It's interesting.'

'Hot and horrible.'

'All those places to explore: abandoned mines and tunnels, ruins of the original inhabitants' gardens...'

'Barren and boring.'

'You could watch the hologram show. There's one about life before Belmor was discovered...'

'What is this fascination with primitive life forms?'

'...and a whole series made after it was colonized: digging the mines, extracting precious elements from the atmosphere; even a funny one about a slave trying to escape!'

'That's not the hologram you want to see. You want to admire Senior Explorer Set.'

'He was a great Explorer.'

'And you think there'll be a hologram on your planet one day: "Senior Explorer Ysdran, Discoverer and Colonizer."'

'Why not?'

Caneesh decided that this wasn't worth an answer.

'One thought about moronic monsters while I'm meditating on the moon of Uturk, and I'm taking an extra week!'

Andrew walked home slowly. Not a great day. He'd kicked the football so hard it had flown over two fences and wedged itself halfway up the Welsh's elegant blue spruce.

Mrs. Welsh had been very polite about it, but she hadn't wanted anyone climbing that perfect tree, so they'd had to go back and get a ladder and a broom. Eventually he'd managed to poke and flip it out.

Mr. Santorini had been nice about where it had landed. But while Andrew was lying straddled across the jagged rocks of the Santorinis' ornamental pond, in freezing cold water up to his shoulders, and wishing he could just leave the stupid ball where it was, he'd suddenly realized that the football was the same shape as the little ship, and started worrying all over again...

Maybe he really was crazy. Truly nuts, round the bend, lock-you-up-in-the-funny-farm crazy. But how could you tell? If you were crazy, wouldn't you be too crazy to know it?

But he didn't think he was. He wasn't doing anything really weird. Apart from seeing aliens.

"It was true," he said to himself. "We had a UFO spying on Earth. Now all I've got to do is figure out what to do."

That was all. Simple. Nothing to it.

Maybe he'd practise his headstands first. Not even alien invaders were going to interrupt his daily routine of headstands and cartwheels – preliminary training for a career as a stunt pilot! Besides, maybe all that blood to the head would make his brain work.

Chapter Three

They'd left the strange solar system. They'd left the strange galaxy. They'd gone back onto the chart exactly where Ysdran had said they would.

'Exactly?' Caneesh asked, as the straight line of the three southern stars was transformed into four stars in an arc. And the Paradise Galaxy…*'Looks like the Galaxy of Despair.'*

Ysdran studied the chart again. *'Never mind, now we know where we are. Just a bit farther out than I thought.'*

'So we're even farther away from home!'

'Only a day… if we stay on Hyperspeed.'

'You know what the Great Thinker thought: "Every day without instruments is a very long day."'

'Which great thinker?' A fat smug feeling oozed its way through the cabin. Ysdran laughed. *'I should have known: the Great Thinker Caneesh.'*

'Who will shortly be meditating in the marsh on the moon of Uturk.'

'Who will,' Ysdran corrected, 'be exploring the ruins of Belmor with the discoverer of another great colony.'

'Great nightmare, you mean!'

They squabbled happily till they touched the borders of the Galaxy of Despair.

'Which is where,' Caneesh began anxiously.

'I know, I know; don't tell me.'

'Rule Six Thousand and Three: I have to remind you that one hundred and thirteen Explorers are known to have died here. Another three hundred and sixty-four have gone missing with a ninety-nine point nine per cent likelihood that they also died here.'

'Thanks, Caneesh.'

'Which makes a total of four hundred and seventy-seven wasted trainings and ships. – And Companions,' he added after a moment.

'And you don't want to make it four hundred and seventy-eight?'

'Don't joke about it! You know what it would mean!'

Ysdran did. And she was close enough to know what the Galaxy of Despair meant, too. Starquest was becoming sluggish and heavy to steer; they were nearing the Great Black Hole.

She tried to stay confident. After all, she knew what to expect: she'd passed her black hole simulator test at her first go. ('A second attempt,' the examiner had said, 'is something a real black hole will never give you.')

That wasn't the only difference. The simulator hadn't given her any idea of the true, greedy power of a black hole. Calculating the safe distance as well as she could, and then doubling it, she'd still brought them within range of its insatiable tug. Her little ship, pointing to the right, was slowly drifting to the left.

'Oh, no, you don't!' she shouted.

'That should change its mind,' Caneesh jeered. 'That's one thing about black holes – they always do what they're told!'

Ysdran ignored him. She was directing all her energy into forcing the ship away from that dangerous pull. It was still only a tug, they weren't inside the true force field, but it was getting stronger. If they didn't get out of it soon they'd be sucked in with a *whoosh!* Sucked in, condensed and gone – faster than the speed of light.

Starquest trembled, torn between the force of her steering and the hungry gulping of the black hole. Ysdran sucked her antennae back into her body. The ship plunged in that split second as she pulled herself in, squeezing as tightly as she could –

– and shot herself forward into one giant

antenna, all her power concentrated on forcing Starquest over. "The Bucket" shuddered again, locked and rocking between two equal forces. Ysdran went on pouring herself into her steering, and tried not to wonder how long she could last.

Suddenly Caneesh joined her. Sliding sideways into her mind, so softly, so smoothly that her concentration was never jarred, he poured his will into hers like a stream joining a creek.

It was enough. Reluctantly, Starquest turned. With one spider-thin antenna, Ysdran flicked the ESCAPE switch.

The ship roared and shot out of range. Moments later, the Galaxy of Despair was behind them. Ysdran pointed back to Cruise and huddled behind her controls, exhausted.

But at least it was pure, simple exhaustion. A little extra helium, a little extra rest, and she'd be back to normal. It wasn't the same for Caneesh. He had a very small amount of energy to last him his lifetime. When it was gone, so was Caneesh.

'How could you do something so dangerous? That's not a Companion's job.'

'What job would I have had in a black hole?'

'A small one.' Ysdran began to giggle and couldn't stop. *'Get it? We'd have been pretty small if it had swallowed us.'*

'I got it.'

Ysdran giggled so hard that little antennae like porcupine quills shot out all over her.

'Hopelessly hysterical,' Caneesh sniffed, *'inanely incompetent blundering buffoon.'*

He went on chanting insults until Ysdran had stopped giggling and lost her quills, and he'd used up all his vocabulary.

'You're right about one thing, though.'

'That you're a dimwitted dreamer?'

'No: about training that alien. I'd better get started.'

The problem with Sunday night, Andrew thought, was that it meant the next day was Monday. School. And school meant deciding: to tell or not to tell.

He'd pictured himself being a hero, but now, after his afternoon with Kerry, he could see another picture – Andrew the loony.

And what about calling the Armed Forces? Phoning the radio and television stations? Protecting the world from alien invasion?

Too late to do anything tonight. He'd decide in the morning.

His mother came in to kiss him goodnight.

"Andy, try not to think about what you saw," she said. "And... promise me you won't tell anyone else about it." She didn't really mean promise, as though he had a choice. "This is an order" was what she meant, do not talk about aliens. Do not even think about aliens.

Sure. That's an easy one.

"Okay," he muttered, keeping his eyes closed. A hint. Mom, I'm going to sleep. No cosy chats.

His dad stuck his head in the door, looking large and embarrassed. "Goodnight, Son."

He hadn't come in to say goodnight for years, and he'd never, ever, called him Son! Andrew had never felt so lonely. He couldn't even smuggle Max out of his basket and into bed with him – the way his parents were acting, they were likely to pop in again to check that he was all right.

'And how am I supposed to not think about the spaceman?' he wondered.

'Ysdran!' a voice corrected, dropping the name into his head right on cue. *'And I am not a space-man!'*

'You're a girl?'

'Quick, aren't you?'

'I don't care what you are! I just want you to get out of my head and leave me alone!'

Her shock was like a pinprick in his brain. *'Don't you want to talk to me?'*

'No! Oh, I don't know. Maybe. I wouldn't mind so much if someone believed me!'

'You can communicate with the other aliens?'

'What do you think? Of course we can – and we do it properly, out loud, not invading each other's heads.'

'Show me.'

He put a picture in his mind of himself talking to Kerry. 'How come you speak English, anyway?'

She couldn't understand that at all. He tried to make a picture of his French class, which didn't help her (didn't help him most of the time, either!), then remembered the time he'd had dinner at Antonio's, when the grandmother and parents had spoken nothing but Italian.

'So you transmit your thoughts in code? Different codes for different groups?'

'I guess so.' He hadn't thought of it like that before. 'But I still don't understand why you speak my language.'

'Because we're not using a code at all. We're simply exchanging thought waves. It's not nearly as complicated.'

It sounded incredibly complicated to Andrew.

'How far away are you?'

Ysdran flicked her mind to Caneesh. 'Approximately eighty-three point five six thousand light years.'

Andrew couldn't remember exactly what a light year was. A long way, anyway.

'So where are you now?'

'Nearly through the Galaxy of Despair, on my way home.'

'Where's home?'

'Rougita, of course! In the Home Galaxy.'

Of course. Rougita. Anyone would have known that. Anyone who travelled around space and met a lot of aliens, maybe.

'You mean you're not from this solar system?'

'Your galaxy isn't even on our charts!'

'So how can our thought waves travel so far?'

'I'm not sure,' she admitted. 'It's supposed to be impossible to thought-share with an alien.'

'But it's how you talk to each other?'

'Yes, but never at these distances. Maybe it happened because our minds touched when we first saw each other. You gave me a terrible shock!'

'I gave you one! I stopped believing in space creatures right after Santa Claus.'

He put a good Santa picture in his mind: red suit, round belly, flowing white beard and bag full of computers; the whole bit.

Ysdran laughed, tickling his mind. 'I've seen those. There's a colony on the Forgotten Planet in the Southern Galaxy.'

'Oh, wow.' Andrew wanted to laugh, too. Laugh or explode or something. 'This is unreal. Unrealer and unrealer. Look, Ysdran; I know you helped me move the pencil. How did you do that?'

'You were already pointing; I made you stronger.'
'But I didn't touch it!'

It was her turn to be puzzled. Puzzled and scornful, as if he'd said something disgusting.

'Why would you want to touch *anything?'* She put a picture into his mind of how she moved, shooting an antenna out of her round, fluid body towards, but never quite to, what she was aiming for. *'But your antennae are always in the same place, aren't they?'* she asked. *'Isn't that awkward?'*

'Isn't it confusing having arms shoot out all over your body?' Andrew retorted. But he still wanted to know how to move things without touching them.

'Just point,' she explained, *'and concentrate.'*

He turned on his bedside lamp. There was a chocolate bar on his desk, waiting for tomorrow's morning break. He pointed at it.

'Harder!'

He concentrated fiercely, straining his arm as though he could reach the desk, not seeing anything in the room except the bar, willing it to come.

It slid slowly along the desk... over the edge... and into the air, inching towards him.

'I'm doing it!' He didn't open his mouth – but he'd broken his concentration. The bar thumped to the floor.

Max was awake in an instant, out of his basket and across the floor. Max loved chocolate.

49

So did Andrew, but not after the dog had got to it first.

He felt a buzzing *ping!* like a brain cell being tweaked. "Ouch!"

'You have to go on thinking!'

Andrew rubbed his head, wondering how he'd bumped it. Ysdran tuned out for a second. When she returned, she was in her cheerful, tickling mood again. *'I can teach you lots of tricks,'* she purred, and her mind rubbed his like a furry cat. *'You'll have to work hard, but you'll like it.'*

Andrew's mind was warm and glowing, and so light that it could have floated away from his neck. He'd never known a feeling like it. Delirious wasn't strong enough. Happy didn't even come close.

*

'That was nauseating.'

'Then don't do it.'

'His mind is all soft and lumpy... unformed.'

'I'm sure that Senior Explorer Set had to make sacrifices, too.'

*

So in the end there was no decision to make. Mom had forbidden him to tell anyone. And even if he told the Armed Forces and they believed him, would it matter? Ysdran was so small and cute and cartoony – how could he have ever been scared of her? She and her spaceship were no danger to anyone.

Maybe he could talk her into coming back and staying with him. His own pet alien. They could do tricks together – real tricks, better than Kerry's mom's – be more famous than Kerry's mom!

*

'What happens if you sharpen your monster's mind enough to figure you out? Lies like that Forgotten Planet full of – what did it call them – Santa Clauses? How in space did you think that one up?'

'He wanted me to. He liked believing it. Anyway, how do you know there isn't a planet like that?'

'True. Nothing could be weirder than that mobile black hole. What are you going to do, use it to mask his mistakes by eating the evidence?'

'You've got to admit it's fast.'

'A space slug is fast compared to the other one! And as easily trained.'

'When did I ever want to do anything easy? But you know that, in the end, I always do what I think.'

Andrew was practising his headstands before school. He could stay up ten minutes now without wobbling. He could even watch TV and follow what was going on. His next goal was doing his homework upside down.

But not this morning. This morning he didn't feel like thinking about anything. Apart from Ysdran, anyway.

'This is awful!' she squealed, squirming around his mind. *'What's happening? I can't think!'* She squirmed worse, and Andrew tipped over.

'That's better! What were you thinking about?'

'Nothing. Just standing on my head.'

'Upside down?'

'I've never figured out another way to do it!'

'But why? Were you being punished?'

'Because I like it!'

'Well, don't do it while you're talking to me. It makes me feel strange.'

'But doesn't your ship ever go upside down or spin around or anything?'

'The ship does. I remain in perfect equilibrium on my atmospheric cushion.'

For a split second she let him see the way she floated, absolutely still, in front of her controls, and then she was gone. He had the feeling she was still annoyed.

'I will not think about Ysdran in school. I will not think about Ysdran...' Andrew walked fast, met Kerry on the way, and heard about the video Kerry had watched last night, so that was okay.

English was okay, because there was a test, and (for some reason that he wasn't going to think about) he'd forgotten about it, so it was pretty hard and there wasn't time to think about anything else.

Geometry was okay because they were doing diagrams, and he couldn't concentrate on anything except working out what the radius was supposed to be, fiddling with the compass and lining up degrees on the protractor.

Lunchtime was okay: no one surprised that he didn't have any news, no one expecting him to have done anything different, everyone too busy telling what they'd done to really care anyway.

But after lunch came History. History was not Andrew's favourite subject. He wouldn't have minded World War II if they'd just studied the planes and left the rest out, but the teacher was keen on dates and reasons and Churchill and Eisenhower.

Did they have to study history on Ysdran's planet? Did they have school? Maybe they just took a pill and learned it all: a history pill, a spelling pill, a how-to-fly-a-spaceship pill...

'Don't be silly – Learning Pills went out of style

eons ago! The only way to learn something compli-
cated is to recharge with helium just before you try
the simulator.'

Maybe history class would be more interesting
if they used flight simulators. Tried being a pilot
in each different Air Force. Which would he
choose first?

"Andrew?"

"Uh. Spitfires!"

Hysterical giggles, from everyone except Mr.
Blake. Jarred roared so hard he nearly made himself
sick. Even Kerry couldn't stop laughing.

'What's going on?' Ysdran demanded.

"I'm sorry, Mr. Blake; could you repeat the
question?" And at the same time, shouting inside
his head, *'Not now, Ysdran! Go away!'*

*

'I don't believe it!' Ysdran fumed. *'He cut me off*
just as I was going to explain why he needs con-
tinual practice! We'd had a perfect lead-up to it.'

'Maybe it doesn't want to be trained.'

'Of course he does; he's perfect for it. He likes it
much better than whatever he was doing then.'

*

A pet alien, Andrew realized, could cause problems. He would have to sort something out. Sometimes he could think about her and nothing happened; other times she appeared as soon as he pictured her. It must be when they thought of each other at the same time. If he was going to persuade her to come back and stay with him, he'd have to teach her to stay out of his mind when he was in school.

'Oh, Space Junk!' Ysdran groaned, staring out of the front windscreen. *'Look what we've got coming!'*

It was a meteor storm. And she was nearly in it. Should she slow down and thread her way through, or speed up and try to escape it?

– Run and shoot out around it. At least that would be exciting. The other way would be just plain terrifying.

'Here we go!' she shouted, and flicked to ESCAPE speed. For a moment she thought they were going to make it – but only for a moment. Only until she realized that every time she got near the edge of the storm another meteor appeared beyond it. And another and another...

So there was no way around terror. No matter which way she turned, she had to fly through the middle of it. Manoeuvre around each meteor.

...Very slowly. Otherwise she was likely to end up on the middle of one of them: a rather unhappy, very dead speck on a rock – which didn't fit in at all with the future she had planned. She turned again, and headed straight into the path of the storm.

'Meteor storms in the Galaxy of Despair,' Caneesh announced, *'are likely to be denser in the other quadrant.'*

Ysdran veered over. The sky began to look clearer. Except for that one... Except for those two...

'Yuck!' she exclaimed. *'We'll never make it between those monsters. They're nearly touching.'* And at that speed, "touch" was not quite the right word. More like "explode."

'Cataclysmic collision.'

'You don't want to see if we'll fit between them?'

'They make the Black Hole look welcoming!'

Ysdran was already swerving. They dived back into the main stream: point and dive, point and swerve; up, down, side to side. The rocks kept on coming. Many were no bigger than her ship, some smaller; all were deadly.

On and on and on.

Finally the cloud in the windscreen thinned to a speckle. A last swerve to the right, another to the

left, a leap straight up – and the sky ahead was clear and Caneesh was rubbing her mind in joy. *'Our chances of reaching Rougita,'* he told her, *'have just been raised to –'*

'I still don't want to know. Not unless it's up to one in a thousand.'

He didn't answer.

"Andrew?" His mother hesitated. "You don't have to go to school today."

Why did he feel that there had to be a catch? And why wasn't she in her Happy Hardware uniform?

"We're going to see a – someone who specializes in talking to kids about problems."

"You mean a psychiatrist?"

"It's just another kind of doctor, Andy."

"I'm not crazy, Mom!"

"Nobody said you were! But sometimes problems that we're hardly aware of can make us react in strange ways... see strange things..."

"I thought Dad believed me!"

"We both believe that you *think* you saw something. But we should find out why you needed to see something like that."

"Because it was there!" Now he knew he was in trouble. He'd shouted at her and she didn't care.

This was serious, and he wasn't going to get a vote.

"It's not easy for us either, you know." Oh, sure. It'd be tough having a crazy kid. His heart bled for them. Or would have, if he hadn't happened to be the kid. "We'll have to leave at ten. You can watch TV for a while."

Wow, what a treat. What did she think he was – five years old? He made a face at her back. He was mad at her, furious with his traitor father, angry at Ysdran. Except that it wasn't Ysdran's fault. It had all been just as big a shock to her as it was to him.

He wondered if she was thinking about him now. If he was crazy, he might as well have some fun.

*

'Ysdran? Ysdran! Ysdran!'

'Don't call so hard... Trying to answer...' Exhaustion blurred her thoughts like static on a radio; he could hardly hear what she was thinking.

'What happened?'

It was too much to describe; she sent him a memory hologram. Without warning he was dumped into the cockpit, while all around him, as far as he could see, was a panorama of hurtling rocks.

As far as he could see: through Ysdran's eye, that wasn't very far. Each meteor loomed up from nowhere into the windscreen in front of him, and then whistled past as a blur of cratered, tortured rock. He felt like a mosquito in a hailstorm, dodging, twisting and turning, wondering where they were all coming from. Then, at last, the relief of empty space, beautiful darkness with only distant stars for company.

'Incredible! I've never seen anything like it.'

There was a pause as Ysdran sucked up a great gulp of helium from her feeder tube. Her energy reappeared instantly.

'It was pretty good, wasn't it?' she boasted. *'Training and concentration – that's what makes me the best. Which reminds me: you're finally ready to do some training, are you?'*

Andrew wondered what she meant by "finally", but it wasn't important. Even her arrogance wasn't important. She had just shown him, as clearly as if he'd been there, a meteor storm in outer space, and nothing else really mattered.

Except for his plan. *'I'm ready,'* he agreed.

They practised for nearly an hour. Sitting cross-legged on his bed, Andrew pointed over a pen, an empty milk glass, and a book.

'I've got it!' he exclaimed.

He turned the light on and off twice; pulled the curtains open and shut and open again. Sent the book and the pen back to the desk.

'Now the glass,' he decided. *'Then I'll get ready for the crazy-doctor.'*

The glass was halfway between the bed and the desk, suspended in mid-air, when his mother opened the door.

"Oh, my God!" she screamed, and slammed it shut again.

'What do I do now?'

'Clean up the mess,' suggested Ysdran.

It took his mother the long drive to the psychiatrist's office to convince herself that she hadn't seen what she'd thought. Andrew had never known her so upset.

He'd never known her to drive so badly, either. "Mom!" he screamed, as they roared up to a red light.

She shouted something he'd never heard her say, the brakes squealed, and they both shot against their seat belts. The car stopped.

The man behind blared his horn, leaning out the window as he swerved around them. "Where'd you get your licence? In a cereal box?"

Andrew wished Ysdran had taught him something useful, like becoming invisible.

The light turned green, and his mother's face turned back to its normal colour. "Sorry, Andy."

"It's okay, Mom." Suddenly he felt almost sorry for her, as if he were the adult here. She'd seen something she didn't understand, and she was as confused as he'd been when he first met Ysdran. "Do you want to know about the glass?"

"No. Not right now. Wait till we get there."

"What's his name?"

"Dr. Lupin."

"Loopy Lupin," Andrew muttered.

"We were very lucky to get an appointment so quickly. It's usually a terribly long wait to get in to a psychiatrist."

Andrew felt so lucky he could hardly speak.

Dr. Lupin's office was in a rambling old house with a high fence and a brass name-plate on the gate.

"What a beautiful place!"

'Fine,' thought Andrew. *'You stay and talk to the doctor about his garden, and I'll go for a walk.'*

"Andrew!" The receptionist smiled as he walked in, as if she'd been waiting for Christmas and he was Santa Claus. "Go on in to the waiting room while I get your mom to fill in some forms."

The end wall was covered by a seaside mural: artistic rocks, golden sand, peaceful white sail boats and sea gulls. The wall opposite was a circus fantasy of prancing horses, vague giraffes, and happy lions jumping through hoops. He quite liked them, especially the beach, but not enough to sit and stare for half an hour. The toys were all babyish and the magazines seemed to be about nothing but the royal family, dieting and chocolate cakes.

His mother was still with the receptionist. How many forms were there?

Here she was. He started looking through one of the magazines as if he'd been doing that all the time.

"Aren't these murals wonderful?" she exclaimed.

"Huh!" Andrew grunted. "Probably a test to see how crazy you are – if you take your clothes off and start swimming, they lock you up."

"Nobody's going to lock you up! I simply think there are times in everyone's life when their problems get too hard to handle, and a psychiatrist can help. There's nothing wrong with that."

"Except that I haven't got any problems!"

"Andrew? Mrs. Shewan? I'm Dr. Lupin." He was tall and grey and bony, with exactly the same expression of vague surprise as one of the giraffes in the mural.

Act normal, Andrew told himself. But normally he just did things; he didn't think, should I smile now? Should I say "hi" or "hello"?

He left his mother, who was looking surprisingly small and tucked-up and anxious, and followed the doctor down to another large room with a desk and two squishy armchairs, a child's pine table and chairs, and a doll's house. A framed photograph of two cats stood on the desk.

"Siamese," Dr. Lupin explained. "Id and Ego; the bigger one is Id. Do you have a pet, Andrew?"

"A dachshund. His name is Max." He could have added more, but pet time was over.

"I hear you've been seeing some pretty strange things lately?"

"Just one."

"A UFO?" Andrew nodded. "And how often have you seen it?"

"Just once. But the alien can talk to me when we both want to."

"Ah." Dr. Lupin nodded understandingly. "When you both want to."

"Yes," Andrew agreed, in his head adding, *'Ysdran! I might need some help!'*

"You're an only child, are you?"

Andrew nodded.

"Any friends?"

"Yes!" What did he think he was?

"Lots of friends, eh? Anyone special?"

"Kerry, I guess. We hang out together."

"Tell me about him – her?"

"Him. I don't know. He has three brothers and four sisters. They all have names like his, names you can have for a boy or a girl. His parents think it's more fair that way. Kerry's brilliant with computers and video games – they're quite rich, so he always has new things like that." He stopped, but

64

Dr. Lupin was still just nodding, waiting for him to go on. "He's smart, too, but not as good at sports as you'd think, considering his dad's a professional golfer."

"Mm, hm."

Great answer. What did this guy want?

"And his mother's a magician; she's on TV sometimes."

"A magician," Dr. Lupin repeated gravely.

Maybe he liked magic!

"Sometimes I go to her show with Kerry. Her tricks are amazing. I mean – I know they're not real, but they look like it on stage."

"Mm, hmm. Would you like to do some drawing for me, Andrew?"

'Not really,' he thought, but it was probably better than talking. "What do you want me to draw?"

"Whatever you want."

Funny how a blank piece of paper in a psychiatrist's office was a lot blanker than a piece of scrap paper at home. He had no idea what he was supposed to do. Finally he drew a plane: a Messerschmitt, because he'd finished a model of one a few days ago.

That was funny, too. A week ago, building a model airplane had been about the most exciting thing in his life. Then he'd met Ysdran... and now here he was, drawing pictures at a kindergarten table and wondering if he'd be asked to play in the doll's house next.

He should have stuck to models.

"You're interested in airplanes, are you, Andrew?"

'How'd you figure that one out, Doctor?' "Yes," he said.

"And what about spacecraft, rockets; you interested in those, too?"

"Not as much as planes."

"Not as much as planes," Dr. Lupin repeated. "And yet it was a spaceship that you say you saw. Can you explain that to me?"

"I guess because it was a spaceship."

"You guess – You're not sure then, are you, Andrew?"

This was getting boring.

'Ysdran!' he called again. This time she was listening.

'I'm ready!'

"Did you ever have an imaginary friend, Andrew?"

"You mean like a little orange alien?"

"Well, yes; I think we'd certainly count that as an imaginary friend. Can you tell me anything about him?"

"Her," Andrew corrected.

'She's a brilliant pilot,' Ysdran prompted.

"She's a brilliant pilot," Andrew repeated. "And very modest."

"Mm, hm."

"She can move things around without touching them."

"That's an interesting talent."

"I can do it, too."

"Mm, hm. And can anyone else see this alien, or just you?"

"Anyone could have, I guess, when she was here. She got scared when she saw Max and me, and flew away."

'A tactical retreat!' hissed Ysdran.

"Sorry," said Andrew.

"Sorry?" asked Dr. Lupin. "For what?"

"For the mess," and Andrew pointed to the desk. He had gradually willed all the pencils, pens and erasers to the edge. Now the entire set of coloured pencils, a fountain pen, two blue pens and two red, floated dreamily across the room and clattered to the floor.

'Brilliant!' cheered Ysdran.

"Mm, hm," said Dr. Lupin.

"I'll get them," offered Andrew. He squatted in the middle of the floor and pointed them all back to him. One by one, like iron filings to a magnet, pencils and pens slithered or rolled from under desk and chairs. The erasers bounced like small eccentric balls from behind the doll's house into his hand. *'Great!'* he told Ysdran. *'Just what the doctor ordered!'* He couldn't help grinning as they all jumped from his hand back to the desk.

"Good boy," said Dr. Lupin. "Now, if you go back to the waiting room, I'll have a little chat with your mother."

"Okay," said Andrew, waving goodbye, and letting the picture of Id and Ego fly gently over the desk to perch on the doctor's left shoulder like a flat-faced parrot.

Chapter Four

He could hear them talking long after he was supposed to be asleep. Long after they were usually in bed themselves. Finally he got up and crept to the living-room door to listen.

"...Made up the alien to give himself power," his mother was explaining. "Also, because he's an only child, he needed to make up a family with lots of brothers and sisters..."

"And more interesting parents than a factory foreman and a sales assistant!"

"That's not true!" Andrew shouted, bursting into the room. "I don't want Kerry's family!"

His father put his arm around him. "We know. Just that crazy man you saw today didn't."

"Didn't you tell him you knew Kerry, Mom?"

"I tried. But he had his theory, and he was going to make everything fit."

"What about the stuff moving around the room?" Andrew asked.

"Moving what?"

His mother looked embarrassed. "I didn't tell you about that, Bob. Oh, Andrew! You didn't do it there?"

"Do what?"

"His pencils wandered around the room for a while," Andrew admitted. "And the picture of his cats... ended up on his shoulder."

"WHAT!"

His mother began to laugh. "That poor man," she shrieked. "He had his nice neat theory: an only child, making up a friend with a fantastic family. Then this over-active imagination combined with your interest in airplanes until you convinced yourself that you'd seen a UFO! When you actually started to show him, he couldn't cope; it was easier not to see it!"

Suddenly she stopped. Her face was pale and tense and she was staring at Andrew as if she'd only just realized who he was. "How do you do it?" she asked.

"You mean you believe me – about Ysdran and the spaceship and everything?" His father shrugged. His mother nodded. "It's like a two-way radio: if we're both tuned in, we can talk to each other. In our heads." For the first time, his parents were listening seriously. "If I'm talking to her, I can do some things the way she does; just sort of point and think."

"Can you show us?"

'You bet!' exclaimed Ysdran, who had tuned in when Andrew mentioned her name.

"I have to concentrate hard," Andrew explained. "I'll turn on the TV." He pointed, turned it on, changed channels, turned it off.

His parents were silent for a long moment. "You've always complained," his dad said finally, "that we're the only people who don't have a remote control. Well, now you *are* one!"

*

'I don't understand,' Caneesh complained. *'Your friend –'*

'Andrew.'

'Andrew seems to be a slave to the bigger aliens.'

'Maybe not quite a slave. Maybe a companion.' And then, as the needles of Caneesh's disapproval pricked at her – *'Not a Companion like you! Primitive creatures would have primitive companions.'*

'But why are the most primitive ones in charge?' Caneesh demanded. *'It's natural that the bigger ones don't perform properly: they haven't been condensed and completed, formed and finished. I can under-*

71

stand that. I just can't understand why they're the bosses!'

Ysdran, scanning the sky in case she'd missed something while she was preoccupied with Andrew, had been wondering too. *'I don't know why they're so dumb,'* she admitted, *'but they're definitely the ones in control. Andrew doesn't feel as if he has any power.'*

'He likes it, though. For example when he played tricks on that other big one.'

'That was the weirdest alien yet! But you're right, it made Andrew feel good. He'll be an ideal assistant when we take over.'

'You think you'll be able to trust him?'

'Of course! He'll love it – he'll be the most powerful slave in their world. And I'll be the most powerful being: Senior Explorer Ysdran, with nothing to do but live a life of luxury.'

'Which would be wonderful – if you didn't despise doing nothing.'

Andrew got up early. He got in touch with Ysdran and made breakfast. His dad grinned as Andrew opened the fridge, poured orange juice and dropped toast into the toaster, all without moving from his chair.

His mother didn't find it so funny, and the tight little smile on her face split into a "Really, Andrew!" as the toast skimmed past her nose on its way to the table.

"You'll sure impress the girls with this, Andy! Who is it you're always talking about – Caroline? She'll notice you now!"

"It's five to eight, Dad."

His father pushed back his chair, gulping the last of his coffee as he pulled on his jacket, made a kissing face in his wife's direction, and rushed out the door.

"It's all right, Mom," Andrew said when he'd gone. "I wouldn't do anything like that."

She tried to smile. "Not even for Caroline?"

Andrew laughed. He wasn't going to commit himself: it was none of their business who he liked. Caroline was smart, but a pain. He wouldn't mind impressing Tracy, though.

'I have a theory,' Ysdran announced. *'If the bigger creatures are in control, they must have had more time to gain power. They must be older.'*

'You mean – they get bigger as they get older?'

'They must.'

It was such a crazy idea that Caneesh couldn't

even imagine it – his mind felt woolly and confused. *'But Rule Number Four says, "All creatures will shrink by one-tenth of their size every century." And the Greatest Thinker of All says, "Great size is a problem, but it will be cured with time." It's a law of the universe, Ysdran: we're large when we're formed, and go on shrinking till we disappear.'*

'It's a law of our universe. It could be different in theirs.'

'But that means they'd go on growing and growing, forever! Getting more and more primitive as they get more and more massive!'

It did sound crazy.

'You'd better find out how long they live,' Caneesh pointed out, *'because the big ones he's shown you look as impossible to train as the mobile black hole. At the rate you're going, your friend will end up the same way before you finish his training.'*

'Andrew!' Ysdran called. *'Andrew!'*

Andrew was in English. He had half an hour left to write an essay on "My Three Wishes for the World," and he couldn't think of one. And now Ysdran was calling him.

'I can't talk to you when I'm in school!'

'I've got a question. Those big ones – the ones that keep causing trouble – have they been formed longer than you?'

74

Big ones that cause trouble. Not a bad way to describe adults. *'Teachers, you mean? And Mom and Dad? They couldn't very well be my parents if they weren't older than I am.'*

'Why not?'

Andrew tried to explain, picturing his parents as they were in the wedding photo in the living room, adding himself as a baby, showing her how he'd grown until now. It wasn't easy explaining human life to someone from another world, and he was pleased with how clearly he'd done it.

'I understand. The blobs –'

'– babies.'

'The babies leave the factory as soon as they're hatched, and go to the parents that the tribe has chosen to look after them.'

'Not exactly.'

'Then where do they come from?'

'Not now!' No way was he going to thought-beam the facts of life through the galaxy, in front of a watching teacher and a waiting paper.

'From the parents?' Ysdran asked incredulously, scurrying around the edges of his thoughts.

'It's not important.'

'I want to know!' Her anger prickled at him. Andrew got hotter and redder and was sure he could feel Mr. Blake wondering why. He bent

down, untied his left shoelace and did it up again, slowly and carefully, tightening at each hole.

'You're upside down again! Stop it! Go back the right way up!'

'When you stop asking about babies.'

'I've stopped! I couldn't think about blobs now if I tried!'

With a final check of his right foot to see if that shoe needed retying too, Andrew straightened up.

Ysdran's confusion was like butterfly wings against his brain. Gradually she returned to normal, and started her next line of attack.

'When will your parents explode?'

'How soon will they die? You ask the weirdest questions, you know that? Not for ages!' He didn't like even saying the word. *'They're not that old – and their parents are still all really healthy. Even Oma, Dad's grandmother in Germany, is all right, and she's ancient. Ninety-two, I think.'*

Ysdran was awed. *'She must be huge!'*

'She is: I've seen pictures. But how did you know?'

'Oops!' Ysdran was gone.

He hoped she wasn't in danger. *'My pet alien,'* he thought fondly. *'No one in the world has a pet like her.'* Except she wasn't in the world, and the thought of that was suddenly so funny it was all he could do not to laugh.

Kerry was staring at him from the other side of the room. Andrew had been evasive about why he'd been away yesterday, and now he could see the hurt behind the freckles.

Slowly and quietly Andrew tore a corner of paper out of his binder. He folded it up, square and heavy, easier to toss. He could throw it; Mr. Blake was probably too absorbed in his pile of marking to catch him. But maybe he just wanted to know if he could do something without Ysdran. A nice simple thing, all on his own.

He held the note in his open palm, and visualized it flying diagonally across four rows of desks to land quietly on Kerry's half-full paper. For a moment he doubted, and it didn't move. Then, believing in it, flying with it, he saw it skim above the heads, hover over Kerry's shoulder, and plop down on the book exactly where he'd imagined. It was so smooth and quiet that Kerry took a second to work out what had happened, and was still staring blankly at his essay when Mr. Blake, with a teacher's sense of missing something he shouldn't have, fixed the class with a cold stare – and went back to his red-penned comments.

Kerry unfolded the paper and read it. His hand came up as if he were scratching his right ear, and gave a quick wave over his shoulder.

*

"So what's the big deal?"

"You know when I told you about the UFO?"

"*That's* the heaps you've got to tell me?"

"Kerry, it's true!"

"Yeah, sure. So's Santa Claus."

Andrew grinned, but kept that secret to himself. Kerry was so used to either watching the tricks behind magic or telling his own incredible stories that now, when something amazing had actually happened, he couldn't see the difference.

"Kerry, did you see how I sent you that note?" For the first time Kerry looked interested. "I sort of – wished it. The alien taught me how."

"Right, Andrew. The alien in the UFO taught you how to pass notes in class."

– Ysdran had tuned in. Andrew felt it like the click of a telephone extension being picked up. *'Show him something good!'*

Something good.

They were nearly up to the football field. The football team was training. Big Luke Williamson, seventy-eight kilos of bully, had the ball. He made a tremendous kick, the kind of boot they knew so well.

'I've only got a second,' Ysdran warned. *'I'm a fraction closer to the Great Chaud Star than I meant to be.'*

Andrew pointed. The ball, checked in mid-flight, rose a metre higher, turned around and flew back the way it had come, over Luke's head and straight through his own goal posts.

The play stopped dead. Kerry's mouth dropped.

"Williamson!" roared the coach. "What do you think you're doing?"

"Believe me now?" Andrew asked.

It was a while before Kerry could speak. "...You really did that, didn't you? You just pointed and... Awesome!"

"Not only pointed – it's more in the thinking."

"So is that what you did yesterday, practise mental aerobics?"

"Not exactly."

"So?"

Andrew hesitated. "My mom took me to a psychiatrist."

"Did he psych out your tricks?"

"He wasn't crazy about them."

"And he found out you were?"

"He said I'd made everything up. Even you."

"Now we know the man's insane!" Kerry said. "You're way too boring to create a fascinating individual like me!" Andrew grinned. That was the nicest thing anyone had said to him since Friday night. "My mom's going to be green – and I mean *lime-jealous* when she sees what you can do."

"Don't tell her," Andrew begged. "I promised I wouldn't tell anyone." He didn't count Kerry. Kerry was his best friend. "We can show her later, maybe."

"Why later?"

"Ysdran might come back to be my pet. Then Mom would have to let me tell people."

"A pet alien! Out of this world! Do you think he –"

"– She."

"...Could bring one for me?"

"I don't know." It wouldn't be so special if he wasn't the only one... But Ysdran might be lonely without anyone else like her around – and he'd still be the first. "I'll ask her."

"Don't worry; I won't be allowed to, anyway. Someone in my family is bound to be allergic to aliens. Hey, look! It's a television van! You're going to be on the News: The Football Finger Kid."

"How could they know?"

"Luke must have figured it out."

"Wish I'd gone to karate when my dad wanted me to."

"Even Luke wouldn't kill you on TV. "

The van cruised past them and turned onto Lookout Road. It was followed by a stream of cars. They were all heading towards the sea. None of the drivers glanced at Andrew.

"Looks like you're not famous, after all."

Another television van went by, closely trailed by cars from *The Daily News* and *The Morning Herald*.

"Must be something big!"

"Maybe your alien's landed again!"

Cars filled the streets as the boys neared Look-out Point. News crews and spectators with binoculars jostled for positions along the cliff-top.

Kerry pushed, shoved and ducked past elbows and video cameras. Andrew stepped quickly through each gap before it closed, and they eventually reached a precarious cliff-front seat.

Look-out Point jutted over the south side of a sheltered cove. The water below was deep all the way to the rocky shore. In the middle of the water, a killer whale was circling slowly. Languidly.

"It looks bored."

"More likely it's hunting something," said Andrew, the self-made whale expert. "But I can't see what... and why is it alone? It should be with its pod."

Suddenly the triangular dorsal fin was raised and the sleek black shape arched. There was a flash of white belly as it dived, the flippered tail flukes disappearing last, like the pointed toes of an elegant diver. Vast and dully black in the blue, the orca sank deeper and became nothing but a dark shadow circling the cove.

"Why is it staying there?"

"Maybe it's sick."

"Maybe it's gone to the bottom to die!"

"Why isn't there a vet here, instead of all these reporters?"

The shadow below them rocked gently in the waves; it might have been a submarine, a shipwreck, a dead thing. The wind was cold on the back of their necks. They were both hungry; Kerry was restless. "How long has it been under?"

"Must be ten minutes."

Then, under the surface, there was a flurry of movement. Waves rippled and splashed. Suddenly a smaller, black-and-white torpedo popped out of the water. Triumphantly, the tall dorsal fin and then the rest of the mother orca's body surfaced beside it.

A cheer echoed across the cliffs. The boys grinned at each other, too elated to be embarrassed about their earlier fears.

"How could it learn to swim already?"

"Not much choice!"

Andrew hadn't noticed Ysdran tuning in. Her mind pricked spitefully at him. *'Is that your Oma? She's enormous!'*

'It's a baby whale.'

'I thought blobs started small!'

83

'It is small – compared to its mother.'

Ysdran felt quite dizzy at the sight of its mother. She took a quick gulp of helium, but the orca remained the same size.

"I'd better go home," Kerry announced, stretching. "We're not going to see much more... unless you can point them over a bit closer to us!"

"I don't think I can move whales around yet! But I'll stay a bit longer, anyway."

Kerry jogged off quickly. His mother would be wondering where he was; Andrew's dad wouldn't be home for another half-hour.

'I've got another question about blobs. Don't stand on your head!'

Andrew promised. Her questions weren't so bad when Mr. Blake wasn't staring at him.

'So: the mobile black hole – the one you call Max – is a baby, and he'll grow as big as the one you call Oma... but this swimming blob is bigger than your father, and it's only just hatched!'

Andrew laughed. His mother called Max a vacuum cleaner, but black hole was even better. The rest of it was so muddled up that he hardly knew where to start.

'Max is a dog! And these are whales! Didn't you notice the difference?'

'You all look the same to me.'

'Ever thought of having your eye tested? We're all

different species! Max won't get any bigger, and – unless he eats an awful lot of doughnuts – my dad can't possibly get as big as a whale.'

'So if you're a different species, why are you so excited about this blob?'

Andrew had never thought about it. What was so exciting about whales? *'They're wild; free. But they're mammals, like us, even though they live in the water. And they're endangered – there aren't very many of them – so it's extra-special to see one. Especially one being born.'*

'How many species does your planet have?'

'Thousands. Probably millions if you count insects and bacteria and everything.'

'Are there many Maxes?'

Andrew had an instant vision of a world overrun by black dachshunds. It was as weird as the Santa Claus planet. *'There are lots of different dogs,'* he explained. *'But you've got a pet, too, don't you?'*

'Companion!' How did he know about Caneesh? She'd never described him.

'Sometimes I can see him when we're talking.'

'I knew that.' And she disappeared again before he could ask anything more.

*

'You know what this means?' Caneesh demanded.

'Don't tell me.'

'Millions of different species, your friend thought. Even if there's only one million, that makes a million-to-one chance that you haven't contacted the most sophisticated. Your aliens are probably already slaves to a superior being on their own planet – maybe to those giant blobs; he said they were free.'

'It's a shame I didn't make contact with one of them. They're already using that hydrogen-oxygen compound.'

'They might not want to share it.'

'Oh, Space Junk!' Ysdran swore. 'Why do things have to get complicated when they seemed so perfect?'

Chapter Five

Despite Andrew's boasting to Kerry, he hadn't asked Ysdran to come back and be his pet. For some reason it never seemed to be quite the right time to say it.

He'd worry about it later. Right now he wanted to think about what he'd done yesterday: changed the course of a ball in mid-flight. That was amazing. It opened up millions of possibilities. It was more than a neat trick: it was a true power.

But how much could he do without Ysdran? He really had to know. The note was the first thing he'd sent on his own.

He wandered out to the back yard. Max jumped up eagerly. "Come on," Andrew called. "Where's your ball?"

It was by the back step: a disgusting-looking, sloppy object, the bright colours slobbered off to a dirty grey. "Yuck, Max! Do I have to touch that?"

The dog pranced hopefully, with a yip to speed him up. Andrew pictured the ball flying from the step and across the yard. He pointed, and the ball flew. Max, still watching his hand, barked impatiently again.

"I've thrown it!" Andrew told him. "It's over there!"

Max refused to believe him.

"I'll bring it back." This time he visualized as he pointed, and the ball flew neatly back to Max's feet. The dog picked it up and dropped it in his hand.

"Believe me now?" Andrew held the ball on his open palm and pictured it flying across the yard again. It flew... tumbled to the ground halfway... and was in the dog's jaws before he could point.

"Give it here, Max," Andrew said, wiping the slobber off on his jeans. He willed it across the yard again.

The ball stayed on his palm. He visualized carefully, willed it... Nothing. He gave it a slight toss in the air, pointed... and the ball landed on his foot. Max retrieved it hopefully.

"So," Andrew thought. "The power's left over from Ysdran. I can do a couple of things, and then it wears off."

He felt disappointed; dissatisfied. A couple of weeks ago he hadn't wanted these powers. Now he was used to them, and he wanted them for his own, not as someone else's leftovers. Not even a pet alien's.

Maybe if he practised harder. Maybe the more he learned the more power he could keep for himself.

'*Ysdran!*' he called, '*Ysdran!*'

*

'*Watch this, Caneesh: my alien is about to find out what training really means.*'

She jumped straight into what she wanted. '*When I met you, there was a lot of hydrogen and oxygen around. Do you know where it was?*'

'*What?*'

Ysdran tried not to transmit her groan, but the effort made Caneesh wince.

'*Hydrogen and oxygen. So much that my instrument meters blew up.*'

'*Exploded? Don't you need them to navigate?*'

'*That's not what we're talking about.*' He mustn't realize how vulnerable she was! '*Please try to concentrate!*'

'*Okay, okay! I just wondered how you got past that Great Chaud Star.*'

'*By concentrating,*' she repeated wearily, like a teacher fed up with a noisy class. '*But now I want to know about your oxygen and hydrogen.*'

'Water? That's H_2O – two hydrogen atoms to one oxygen.'

'I was sure that was what the meter said, just before it blew! And you have a lot of this water?'

'The ocean's full of it. And rivers, taps, rain. It's all over.'

'And there's twice as much hydrogen as oxygen?' She sounded disappointed.

'What's wrong with that?'

'I was just surprised.'

Andrew immediately felt guilty. There were so many things he wanted to know about Rougita – how could he snap at Ysdran for being curious too?

'I think air's mostly oxygen,' he offered. 'I'll look it up.' He flipped through the science encyclopedia on his desk and discovered how wrong he was. 'Air is only twenty-one per cent oxygen; the rest is mainly nitrogen.' He could feel her thinking about that.

'Your planet must be hot,' she decided. 'Too hot for Rougitans to survive unprotected.'

'You'd have to wear sunglasses!' The thought of Ysdran in shades made him giggle. How about in a bikini... lying on a beach towel?

Ysdran didn't see the joke.

Andrew asked, 'Do you have a space suit for when you're not in your own atmosphere?'

'We couldn't have coloni– I mean visited – all the

90

planets in our galaxy if we didn't have efficient atmosphere packs.'

'So you'll be okay if you come back... You will come back?' A warm glow spread over his mind. She was happy. She'd wanted him to invite her! *'What should I do?'* he asked.

'Start collecting oxygen.'

'What?'

'It's all around you!' she prickled. *'You just thought so! Surely you know how to collect it – from the air, at least, if it's too much trouble to separate it from the water molecules!'*

'Oh, sure. From the air, that makes it easy. I do it all the time: put a little hydrogen in my desk drawer, stick the nitrogen in the cupboard... Easy!'

'I don't want nitrogen. And we won't worry about the hydrogen right now: just oxygen!' Sarcasm obviously didn't work across the light years.

'It's in the air, Ysdran; it's not the sort of stuff you can see or do anything with.'

'You can't see it?' She sounded so despairing that he felt guilty again.

'Nobody can.'

'Try,' she encouraged. *'Let me try with you. Concentrate.'*

Concentrate on air. It's not easy. Wherever you look, there's something on the other side. How can you stare at nothing?

'Concentrate with me. Look through my eye.'

Was the air becoming thicker – or were his eyes blurring with effort? Maybe it *was* the air...

The phone rang.

"Hey, Andrew – you want to come over? I've got a new version of that Alien War game."

"Uh, I don't know."

'Concentrate!' hissed Ysdran. *'You've got oxygen all around you – can't you see it?'*

"I'd better check."

'Check! What are you going to check? You're training!'

"Kerry – Mom says I've got to clean my room now, since I didn't do it last weekend." At least the last part was true.

"Okay." Kerry's voice was flat and disbelieving. Not surprising, considering that he knew what time Andrew's mother came home.

"She came home early; she's not feeling well."

That was better, at least on Kerry's side; from Ysdran he was getting a sharp buzzing of anger.

'Shut him off! We've got work to do!'

"See you tomorrow."

"Yeah. Say hi to Max."

Andrew laughed and hung up, trying not to feel like a traitor.

'Oxygen!' he heard again. *'Just look at the air!'*

He fixed his gaze on a square bit of wall – about the only space in the kitchen where there was nothing extra to get in the way. He'd never really looked at the wall before. The paint was cream-coloured; when he studied it he could see the faint texture of the brush marks. And the oil stain like a giant teardrop...

'Not the wall!' Ysdran snarled. *'You've missed the air completely. Don't throw your eye so far!'*

He imagined holding a book in front of him, and tried to focus on where he'd be reading. This time it was definite: the air was thickening and blurring.

"I'm home!"

It was like being woken from a dream: he floundered and struggled and didn't know where he was or what he was doing.

"Andrew? Are you there?"

"In the kitchen."

"Are you all right? You look a bit pale."

"I'm all right." And he would be, if the room would stop spinning. "Actually, Mom, I might lie down for a bit."

She felt his forehead. "Good idea. Call me if you need anything."

"I'll be okay." He made it to his bedroom, and onto his bed. The dizziness faded slightly when he lay down.

'Do you think we could get on with it?'

'She's my mother, Ysdran! I do have to talk to her, you know!'

'Fine. You've talked to her. Now we're thinking about oxygen.'

So he tried again. He had a better idea of what he was doing now, and it didn't take long to get back to the point that the phone and then his mother had interrupted. The air was hazy, like smoke or fog.

'Now look at the molecules!'

'You can't see molecules, Ysdran!'

'You *can't see molecules,*' she corrected. '*I can. So look with me.*'

Suddenly – '*This is* incredible!'

In the space before his eyes, millions of molecules were dancing. They looked exactly like they did in science books – and nothing like that at all. Because these were real, and three-dimensional, and moving. And because it was so impossible that he could be seeing them, just like this, bouncing in front of his eyes.

'They've been there all the time – you've just been too lazy to look.'

He ignored her. This was too amazing to worry about insults.

'That was the easy part,' she went on. 'Now you've got to identify the oxygen and collect it.'

Part of Andrew's mind told him that was crazy. Wouldn't he die if he took the oxygen out of the air?

'Don't be so greedy – you've got lots of it!'

That was true. Looking through her eye, he recognized the oxygen molecules easily: pairs of shimmying atoms, jostling their way through the crowded atmosphere. There were so many that it didn't seem to matter that they were outnumbered four to one. For the first time Andrew understood the meaning of infinity.

Besides, he was too excited to go on questioning. It was easier to do what he was told. Narrowing his concentration further, he focused on one molecule, following it as it roamed through what he'd thought was the still air of his bedroom.

'Now catch it!' The molecule was floating towards the door. Andrew stood up obediently. *'Don't chase it; call it to you!'*

But it was too late. The world had gone black. Andrew had stopped seeing atoms, stopped being obedient, and fainted.

*

'He's gone into shut-down!' She was so angry she could hardly think. *'How could he do that to me?'*

'Maybe it doesn't want to be a slave,' Caneesh

suggested, his jealousy creeping around the cabin like a sulky porcupine. Ysdran ignored it.

'He's too primitive to be worried about that. Besides, he likes the training.'

*

He was drowning in a deep black sea. Waves were lapping at his face; he clutched at a passing dolphin and was towed to the surface, but he was slipping, the dolphin was trying to shake him off...

Andrew opened his eyes. Max was struggling in his arms, whining and licking his face. Andrew let him go.

He'd fainted! But not for very long. He could hear his mother in the kitchen, and it didn't sound as if his dad was home yet. He must have been out for only a couple of minutes.

What happened?

'Ysdran!' he thought, and immediately wondered if you could cancel a thought. He was awake now, but he felt terrible. He did not want to talk to Ysdran.

He didn't want to see his mother, either. Not while he was lying on the floor. Although it was quite nice on the floor, really. His body said it was very comfortable there and it didn't ever want to move again, thanks, but his brain said that it would get taken to a doctor if it was caught there, and his body finally agreed to climb onto the bed.

Max jumped up beside him and rested his long black nose on the pillow. Andrew's mom might have something to say about that, too, but not as much as she would about being knocked out by Ysdran.

"Good dog, Max," Andrew whispered, and plummeted into sleep.

Ysdran waited till she felt his mind rise close to the surface of consciousness before beginning a gentle pricking at its edges.

Andrew peered sleepily at his watch. *'Six o'clock! Ysdran, I need to sleep.'*

'You need to train!'

'I'm not doing it anymore.'

There was a burning flash of anger, as if a fire had exploded inside his brain and been immediately extinguished.

In the spaceship, ferocious waves of tension quivered in Caneesh's mind as Ysdran fought for self-control. She didn't want Andrew to shut down again. Until he was better trained, she'd have to block her anger from him.

Andrew, now that he'd had a moment to consider his decision, knew it was right. She could still come and be his pet, and talk to him from her spacecraft, but his mind was his own. Tricks were one thing; losing consciousness was another. For

98

that short while, he'd had no control over his own body. He'd been totally powerless. It was not something he wanted to repeat.

He hoped she wasn't upset.

*

Caneesh, unable to defend himself from the force of Ysdran's thoughts, concentrated on not thinking about the moon of Uturk.

...But he wished he were there now.

'I haven't given up yet, Caneesh! I'll get him back!'

How had that wish slipped past his guard?

Andrew cleaned his room before he went to see Kerry. He never liked lying.

"What's the new game like?"

"Fantastic, at least for mere mortals who don't have live aliens to play with."

After that, there was no way that Andrew could tell him about the things Ysdran had shown him. Besides, for the moment, he was happy simply pitting his skill against the computer in exactly the same way that he would have a month ago. And happy to forget that, no matter how brilliant these graphics were, they couldn't compare to the feeling of steering a spaceship through a real meteor storm.

It was a good thing that this one wasn't for real: with a burst of flame, he lost his final life and Earth's last chance to be saved from alien invaders. He handed the controls back to a smirking Kerry.

"That noise goes right through one ear and gets stuck in the other," Mrs. Milton complained. "Time for some fresh air, boys. Andrew, you look awfully pale."

"His mom was sick yesterday. He's probably giving us all some deadly germs."

Andrew went from pale to tomato. "She's all right now."

Chased outside, they wandered back to Andrew's house to get Max. The dachshund greeted them with squeaking gifts of licks and bounces, nearly as many for Kerry as for Andrew.

"You'd better be careful, Andy," his father warned. "You get too busy with other things and your dog's going to move in with your friend."

Too busy with your alien, he meant. It was hard to know if he was joking or not.

"No fear!" Andrew retorted, clipping on the leash. He could manage two pets easily. Ysdran hadn't contacted him since this morning, but he didn't feel ready to talk to her, either. There wasn't anything wrong; he just wasn't in the mood. "We're going to Look-out Point to see if the whales are still there."

Judging by the size of the crowd, they were.

*

It had been a long day, and it had taken most of it for Ysdran to recover her temper.

Caneesh had struggled to control his thoughts while he waited for peace, but two more visions of the moon of Uturk had slipped into the cabin before he could stop them. He'd reeled them back in so fast they'd blurred, but he was worried. This had never happened to him before, and since he didn't want to make Ysdran any more tense than she already was, he was trying very hard not to let the worries spill over, too...

'We'll get home, Caneesh.'

He'd been partly successful: she'd picked up the worry but not what it was about.

'Of course we will! With a creative Companion like me, success is ensured.' His thin mind rubbed the sharp angles of hers, and they both began to relax.

'I didn't think he'd be able to shut down like that.'

'It could be a nuisance.'

'He's probably learned his lesson by now. He'll be worrying about why I haven't called him.'

'He doesn't seem to be calling you, either!'

Ysdran ignored that; she preferred to picture Andrew waiting miserably for her to call. Andrew spellbound by the scraps of information she fed him. Andrew thinking that she was the most exciting thing that had ever come into his life.

'I'm a bit confused,' Caneesh lied. *'Who is it that's miserable?'*

'I don't want to upset him too badly... I'll see if he's in a more reasonable mood yet.'

*

The rest of the pod had appeared today; there were six orcas gambolling freely in the straits beyond the sheltered cove. The mother and new-born calf stayed on the edge of the group, another whale hovering like a bossy aunt. The others seemed so happy, spraying and breaching, slapping mammoth tails to make monster waves, that Andrew didn't believe it could be any kind of useful hunting behaviour, and decided that they were simply playing.

"Or showing off for the new baby," Kerry suggested.

Andrew was doubtful. "I wish I knew more about them."

'So do I.'

He didn't like talking to Ysdran when he was with Kerry. *'Later.'*

'One question?'

'As long as it's not too hard.'

'What do they do with that oxygen compound?'

'Live in it: eat, swim, sleep, have babies... what they're doing now.'

'They don't collect the oxygen, store their surplus supplies?'

'I don't think that's the way whales work. They just live!'

'No technology?'

'No possessions!'

'So they're inferior to you?'

'Some people think they might be smarter.'

'But you don't control them?'

'Why would we want to control whales – even if we could? Anyway, I said one question.'

"You need your ears checked, Andrew! I said they're selling hamburgers in the parking lot – do you want one?"

The whales had moved farther out. They looked no more than shapes that could have been shadows, an occasional jet of water that might be the splash of a tail – or reflected sunlight.

"Get three. Max is starving!"

Chapter Six

'*Your* alien doesn't seem to mind that he's missing you miserably.'

'*He would if I stayed away longer.*'

Caneesh began to hum, '*Soon I'll see my red Rougita, Queen of colonies, home to me.*'

Ysdran shrank back inside herself, subdued. Caneesh continued, more forcefully, '*Soon I'll be in sweet Rougita...*' before relenting. '*Some species may be simply untrainable. That's no fault to the Explorer who discovers them.*'

'*No gain, either.*' She had shrunk and shrivelled; her energy had dimmed to a dull glow. Caneesh rubbed her mind, soothing, comforting, until she plumped back to her normal size and brilliance. '*If I'm nice enough to him, he won't even know he's training!*'

*

Andrew was Sunday-morning-dozing, half
awake and enjoying having no reason to get up.
Feather-soft, Ysdran began to tickle the edges of his
mind. The feeling left him warm and happy, as if
he might laugh or sing, ready to face the world –
and breakfast.

'What do you eat?' he asked curiously.

The Energy Outlet was a long tube dangling to
one side of her controls. Swivelling on her
atmospheric cushion, she demonstrated a quick
gulp. *'Long drinks break my concentration,'* she
explained. *'I always store up as much as possible
before I fly.'*

*'That'd be handy: eat heaps today and don't
bother tomorrow – like a camel! What does it
taste like?'*

She inhaled again, holding the taste in her mind
until he could feel it. Taste was harder to read than
pictures, but suddenly he could do it, imagining
that he was putting something into his mouth,
exploring the sensation...

It was exactly like the smell of a week-dead fish.
Andrew choked and gagged. *'That's disgusting!'*

'You don't like it? Try this.' And before he could
turn his mind away she shot another taste image
into it. He was getting better at it – this time he

could smell *and* taste it. He barely made it to the bathroom in time. *'You don't like that one either?'*

'No. I've got the idea, though; don't give me any more!'

'But there are so many flavours to imagine. There must be some you'd like!'

'I'll stick to Earth ones, thanks... Do you just use that one tube, and imagine whatever taste you want?'

'It's a lot better than tasting boring old helium all the time!'

At least that was one thing his mother never made him eat! But there were plenty of other boring things around. So he tried Ysdran's technique at breakfast. His bran flakes turned into butter-crunch ice cream; toast with peanut butter became chocolate cake. With a bit of practice, he might even be able to make liver edible. Since they had liver once a week, that would be the best thing he'd ever learned!

But it was still just a trick. Fun, but not great. Great was that afternoon, when he realized that he could actually train his body by thinking through what he wanted it to do.

Kerry had talked his dad into taking them to the roller-skating rink. Neither of them was good enough to bother buying in-line skates, but it was something to do on a grey spring Sunday.

They started off in their usual style: wobbling, ankles in, arms flapping. After making it twice around the rink without falling, they picked up some speed and confidence. "Race you!" Kerry shouted suddenly, and took off. Wheels whirred; they reached the end of the rink together and crashed, sprawling heavily across the floor.

"Why'd you do that?"

"Idiot."

Three girls circled them, giggling. The boys scrambled to their feet and skated on, trying to look cool. A guy with in-line skates flew past them, dressed all in black, hands behind his back, fast and smooth as an arrow.

"Look at him go!"

Andrew looked. Stared. Studied the man's movements till it was as though he could see them in slow motion. He imagined himself moving like that, pictured the movement of his legs, his arms, the way to hold his shoulders, his head. Everything.

"I can do that," he said suddenly.

Kerry gave him a look that didn't need words.

Andrew leaped forward. The feeling was tremendous. Unbelievable. He didn't worry about falling; he didn't worry about looking stupid. He let his body move the way he'd pictured it, the way the speed skater moved, and it flew him

across the floor. He whirled around the rink, between two of the girls, and flashed to a stop in front of Kerry.

"Let's go home," Kerry said.

Andrew didn't want to go home. He wanted to skate forever. He wanted to keep on flying, to feel the floor melt beneath his wheels.

Or maybe it hadn't been like that. Maybe it had all been in his head. Maybe he'd made a real idiot of himself again.

"Kerry," he said hesitantly. "Was I really skating out there? I mean – did it look as good as it felt?"

"It was good. If I were you I'd start begging for blades for my birthday."

'You see? It was simple. Lots of things are, once you try.'

'Did you help me skate?'

'I helped tune your mind. You did the rest.'

'What do you do for fun on Rougita?'

It took Ysdran a minute to understand. She'd assumed that physical exertion like skating must be some kind of training task, and was annoyed to find herself wrong. As an Explorer, of course she was allowed "fun": three times per decade, in a proper holiday place. Rougita was home – a planet for

110

work and worship – not for fun. And why would a primitive species need pleasure at all?

Finally she showed him her hologram of a storeroom packed with frozen blocks of precious elements.

'What's fun about that?'

'I like imagining that I have them.'

On Tuesday night, Andrew was supposed to be doing geometry homework. Instead he was wondering why Tracy, who'd never even noticed that he was alive, had decided to stack his binder, pencils, compass and rulers on top of her desk so that every time he wanted something he had to snatch it when Mrs. Ellis wasn't looking, while Tracy pretended to ignore him and moved it out of reach.

Two more weeks till the school dance. He wondered if Tracy was going. He might ask her. Not ask her to go! Just ask if she was going. And then maybe they could dance together. A slow dance.

'Yuck! Touching antennae! What are you thinking about?'

'Never mind.'

'But you don't touch antennae with that other one – Kerry!'

'No kidding.'

'And there's a different feeling in the way you think about her.'

'It's not your business, Ysdran!'

'Almost like you're upside down again.'

'Great idea.' Andrew got up and went out to the hall. There was just enough room between his bedroom and the living room to do one cartwheel. And another one back. And another...

'Okay, you win! You can think about that one any way you like! Just stop spinning!'

*

'You know what the Great Thinker thought?'

'Not another Great Thought, Caneesh!'

'"A spinning slave is as useful as sunrise in a black hole."'

Ysdran moaned. 'Don't even think about spinning!'

'Okay. What about "revolving rebel"? "Gyrating giant"? "Whirling..."'

'Stop!'

Tactfully Caneesh changed the subject. 'I've heard that the south end of the moon of Uturk is the most restful.'

Ysdran groaned again.

Thursday was Phys. Ed. and Mr. Armstrong's own special torture session. They were vaulting the horse – or falling off the horse, or killing themselves in the most embarrassing way ever invented, trying to get over the horse. Anyone left alive was rewarded with a rope climb.

"God, I hate this stuff!" Kerry groaned. "But wouldn't it be fantastic to be able to do it once, just to see old Strong Arm's face?"

There was a resounding Thump! from the mat on the far side of the horse. Antonio lay sprawled peacefully on his back, gazing up at the ceiling.

Jarred groaned. "Couldn't you borrow your mom's magic wand?"

Antonio was allowed to sit down and miss the rope climb. That was one way out.

And the other way...

It was Luke Williamson's turn. If he hadn't been such a bully, you'd have had to admire him. He'd been able to vault the horse since he was born. Since kindergarten, anyway.

Andrew stepped out of the line to watch. Watch how fast Luke ran, how he hit the springboard, touched, leaped, landed. Concentrating; concentrating.

Kerry ran, and actually made it over. Not beautifully, not painlessly, but made it.

Mr. Armstrong looked at him as if he were a spider that badly needed stepping on.

"Next!"

Andrew ran. Ran like Luke had. Hit the springboard the way Luke had; grabbed the handles; over... He'd made it!

Made it all right, too, by the look on Armstrong's face. But not well enough to skip the climbing. There were four ropes; Jarred, Kerry and Andrew were the last group.

With a mighty six-inch leap, Jarred grabbed his rope, swung wildly, and thumped to the floor.

Kerry eventually scrabbled up to within an arm's length of the top. He came down quite a lot faster than he'd gone up, and limped away, flapping a bleeding hand.

Andrew was still stuck at the bottom.

"I don't understand this," Mr. Armstrong began, slowly and clearly, as if it were a fight even to get the words out. "A group of twelve-year-old-boys, some perfectly ordinary fitness tasks – and I end up with a bunch of... chattering jellyfish!"

The class looked at their toes and tried to look as unjellyfish-ish as possible.

"Stand aside, Shewan!" the Strong Arm bellowed. "Now, all of you: watch how this is done!"

'If he wants to see a chattering jellyfish,' Andrew thought, *'he ought to meet Ysdran.'*

'Why?'

'Not now – I want to watch this.'

114

The man was good. He ought to have been in a jungle somewhere, playing guerilla warfare – or just plain gorillas. His skills were wasted teaching Grade Seven Phys. Ed.

"Now, Mr. Shewan!"

He thought it through, pictured his own body doing it.

"Andrew Shewan – is anyone home?"

There was. And it worked. He wasn't as fast as the Strong Arm, but he was better than anyone else in the class, even Luke.

And then the finale. Without even pointing, simply staring, as Andrew reached the top of his rope he willed open the shackle of the rope beside him. It hit the wooden floor like a drumstick on a kettle drum, and lay still, snaked across the gym.

Then he undid the other two.

The class had squealed and jumped when the first rope crashed. As the other two thumped down they stood silent and tense, staring at Andrew in his rope perch, high above them.

Mr. Armstrong was white. "Careful, Andrew," he called. "Come down nice and slow." He circled below, as though he would somehow be able to catch Andrew if the last rope fell. "Move those mats," he ordered the boys behind him. "Quietly."

They moved on tiptoe, with the silent, exaggerated care of actors in an old black-and-white movie. Andrew, gazing down at the semicircle of upturned faces, felt removed, isolated, as if he were separated from them by much more than the height of the gym.

Finally, hand over hand, hardly burning his palms at all, he came down. Mr. Armstrong remembered to breathe again. "All right, son?" he asked, putting his arm around Andrew's shoulders.

"Sure," Andrew said, more casually than he felt. "My rope was okay."

"Class dismissed," said Mr. Armstrong.

The tension broke. Boys exploded as loudly as the rope had hit the floor – in the history of noisy, excited changing rooms, this was the noisiest.

"That was the weirdest thing I've ever seen – gave me the creeps!"

"You sure were lucky, Shewan!"

"Lucky? He just did what I told him – borrowed Kerry's mom's magic wand."

"You could have been killed."

"Anyone could! I was the last one up that end rope. If it had fallen then..."

"Lucky, wasn't it?" Kerry said drily. "And lucky that the ropes didn't hit anyone when they fell, too." He finished tying his shoes and walked out.

Andrew let him go. The others didn't notice. They were too busy discussing Mr. Armstrong's face and what their parents would say about unsafe gyms and whether you could sue a school if you didn't actually get hurt, and "*did you see those ropes crash!*"

The mood slipped away as the changing room emptied; now he was trudging home, bored and restless, wondering what had made him do something so stupid – and knowing that, if Kerry hadn't gone ahead without him, that sour energy could have spurted into a fight.

'*The one who doesn't like jellyfish: was he being punished?*'

'*I didn't mean to punish him! It was just a joke.*'

'*A joke can be a very effective way to gain control,*' Ysdran agreed.

Chapter Seven

Caneesh had filled the cabin with a scene of the orange slime-caves on the moon of Uturk. *'Oh, peaceful paradise,'* he sang. *'Oh, marvellous moon!'*

'I've won. I've won. I've won!' Ysdran interrupted, tickling his mind the way he especially hated. *'The alien likes power; he wants control; the rest is simple.'*

Caneesh tried to ignore her, but was not strong enough. The orange slime-caves disappeared.

Andrew had never been a hero before. He was float-in-the-sky high, bouncy and punchy with the adrenaline of the moment.

'Ysdran!' he called, *'Ysdran!'*

The first wisps of green gas had floated by aim-lessly and harmlessly, an hour ago. She'd changed course, but they'd appeared again – in every wind-screen, from every direction – she didn't know where they were coming from. Now they had grown from swirls to a blanketing, bubbling, green fog.

Andrew felt tension, and fear. *'Don't distract me!'* he heard. *'I'm trying to see!'*

Something didn't make sense. At first they'd only connected when they were thinking of each other at the same time. Now they were intruding on each other's thoughts whenever they called, picking up whatever the other was seeing... and feeling.

It was getting stronger – whatever it was.

Green filled the universe; it went on forever. It was worse than the comets or meteors or even the Galaxy of Despair. With those she hadn't had time to worry; she'd pushed the terror to the back of her mind and flung herself into the challenge of pitting bare skills against a universe.

This was different. How could she challenge what she couldn't see? She was close to panic, close to disintegration. Blind, bumbling, edging through with no idea if she was going the right way... *'If only I could see something,'* she moaned. *'Anything!'*

In that instant the clouds vanished and she was staring at the rocky, purple surface of Planet 16A of the Seventeenth System.

'Anything but that, I meant!'

'It might be the sight that saves us. But you decide: do we stay lost or land?'

'Okay, okay; we're going down. Do we know anything about it?'

'Apart from that it has to be better than the last place you tried to land?' Caneesh dredged his memory for the planet's file. *'"16A has been well charted and explored. It has no useful minerals. Exposure to its gas clouds causes instant death. Landing on this planet is forbidden except in case of dire emergency."'*

Ysdran pointed and eased Starquest slowly down to the surface. *'What exactly does "dire" mean?'* she asked. *'Because all I know is that we'll never get out of here if I don't stop to refuel.'*

'Ysdran!' Andrew called again, later that afternoon. *'Ysdran – can you talk now?'*

Nothing. No "Go away, I'm busy"; no sign that anyone was listening at all. He kept on trying, with

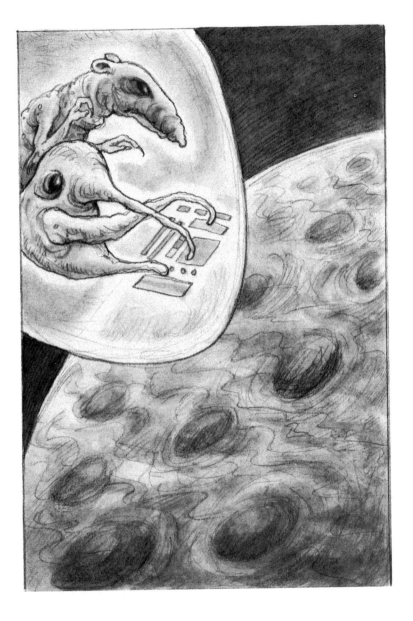

the memory of her panic cramping like a knot in his own stomach. What had that green gas been? Was she still in it? More important, was she ever going to get out?

For the first time it struck him how incredibly tiny her spaceship was. Teeny. Microscopic. Much too little to zip across galaxies, hurtling from one danger to another.

And there was nothing he could do to help. He was absolutely useless, and he'd go crazy if he sat around thinking about it any longer.

He grabbed Max's leash; the dg had sensed his restlessness and was already waiting at the door. "I'm going for a walk, Mom!"

They headed towards the sea. He felt more hopeful just being outside. Maybe his call would be clearer out in the open. And maybe it would be lucky to stand right where he had when they first met. It would be a sign: if he could find the spot, he would reach her; if he could reach her, she'd be safe.

It was a cold day, and getting dark; he and Max had the windy strip of bush to themselves.

Suddenly Max started acting strange. His busy, cheerful trot had slowed when they reached the park, but as they neared the centre area, head and tail were both drooping and he started to whimper.

Andrew dragged him along. Behind that dog-wood was the spot; he was sure of it.

The dog refused to move. Planting his stubby legs firmly on the ground, he skidded, then reared back, yelping and dancing on his hind legs. He'd remembered better than Andrew; this was the place. His yelping crescendoed.

Andrew took him out of the "Scary Zone" and tied him to a tree. Max began to howl.

Andrew stood in the spot where he'd first seen Starquest. He pictured his call as an arrow and shot it through space. *'Ysdran! Ysdran!'*

The only answer was the baying of an unhappy dachshund.

*

Ysdran was in shut-down. Her body was shapeless and relaxed, her mind out of reach.

Caneesh was keeping vigil, constantly scanning the windscreens, checking his own circuits and combing his memory. He didn't know exactly what he was afraid of – he just knew that he felt more worried and miserable than a Companion was supposed to be able to feel.

'She was right to land,' he reassured himself, *'we're not breaking the rules,'* but that reminded him of just how dire this emergency was. Without

instruments, it was going to be nearly impossible to navigate back through that foul green fog. Their only chance was to have Ysdran supercharged, her senses sharpened with excess energy.

He hoped it was enough. The Company's rules were very clear: "There is no excuse for failure. An Explorer who does not survive her first mission has wasted the Company's time and wealth. Her name will be deleted from the Ship of Fame and never thought again. Her tribe will be given three days to pay for the loss of the ship."

And the nightmare of all Companions: "The tribe of a failed Companion will pay a Shame tax for three generations."

'Rest, Ysdran,' he willed. *'Rest and refuel to get us through the foul fog and home to our own perfect planet.'*

And even though she was in shut-down, far beyond the reach of his thoughts, he blocked the rest. Blocked his wondering whether he'd be strong enough to support her. Whether he'd still be with her if she ever did make it home.

*

Andrew didn't know how long he'd been standing there, but it was dark and he was cold, and Ysdran hadn't answered. He untied Max, who

125

was still howling, and ran home as fast as he could, the dog lolloping ahead of him.

Dinner was ready, and his mother was looking worried. "You've been gone nearly two hours! Where've you been?"

"Just down at the park."

"Well, be careful! You can meet some pretty funny people there this time of night."

"Pretty funny not-people too, eh, Andy?" his dad asked, slapping him on the back. "So – what tricks have you got for us tonight?"

"None."

"No tricks?" His dad looked crestfallen. His mother looked relieved.

"I can't get hold of Ysdran."

"Never mind; maybe later."

"And for now," said his mom, "just pass these plates by hand, like an ordinary mortal."

Andrew did the dishes; did a sheet on fractions; watched TV; smiled at his father's heavy-handed jokes; went to bed. Nothing seemed real; only half of him was there. The other half was floating in space, searching for an orange alien that looked like a jellyfish.

He wouldn't sleep. He should keep calling all night. But it had been a long day, and after a last try at midnight, he closed his eyes.

'Andrew? Andrew!' Her voice was sharp and clear, but he was always a slow waker, sitting up in bed and rubbing his eyes before he knew what was happening. *'Andrew! Did you want to think with me?'*

'Ysdran! Where are you?'

She looked out the windscreen and let him see for himself: cratered purple rock and wisps of slimy green gas. Not a nice place for a picnic.

'I thought you were dead!'

'I was in shut-down: like dead, except that I can come back when I'm ready.'

'I'm glad!'

'Why?' she asked. *'No one would know about you – you couldn't be penalized.'*

'Penalized?'

'For the waste.'

'That's horrible!'

'It's Rule Three Hundred and Twelve,' she answered, as if that were the end of any possible argument. *'But you haven't answered my question: why do you care if I survive?'*

It was much harder to lie by sending thoughts than by talking. "I don't know," he would have said, if Kerry had asked him the same question. *'I like you,'* he had to admit now.

127

Ysdran played with this idea. It was not easy for her to understand.

'Like I like Max.'

'You think about me in the same way as that mobile black hole?' She didn't seem flattered. *'I'm going to shut down again. I'll call you when I come out.'*

"Ysdran's all right!" he announced at breakfast.

"That's nice." His mother sounded as enthusiastic as if he'd said that Luke Williamson was coming for dinner.

"So you can do your tricks again? Send me the peanut butter."

"Just pass it!"

His dad winked. Andrew passed the jar by hand, which was probably all he could have done anyway. Ysdran had sounded too weak last night to send anything more than her own thoughts.

"Eight o'clock!" His father grabbed his wallet and keys, threw on his jacket, and raced out the door.

His mother always got ready more calmly. This morning, though, she was thinking about something else. She smacked Max as if it were his fault she'd tripped, and now she was still rushing and it was twenty past eight. "I hate coming home to the breakfast dishes!"

"I'll do them."

"Not unless you do them normally. No alien tricks!"

Andrew shrugged. "Okay."

"Look, Andrew, it's not the dishes. I'm worried about you. Don't get too involved with this alien: I don't think it's healthy."

"I'm not too 'involved', Mom! I'm fine. Anyway, it's twenty-five past eight."

She flew out the door. Andrew rinsed the dishes and dumped them in the draining rack. He was steaming hotter than the water. She couldn't even use Ysdran's name! Showed how much she tried to understand.

"My mom's going nuts this morning," he told Kerry later. "She thinks I'm going to catch some weird space disease!"

"Like what?"

"I don't know. She just said it wasn't healthy."

"Moms can be weird," Kerry agreed, though his wasn't strange in any of the usual ways. You could simply never guess how she was going to react to anything. "Couldn't I tell her about the alien?"

"Her name's Ysdran," Andrew snapped. "No; I told you. Not yet." The look on Kerry's face told him how he'd sounded. "She's sort of sick," he explained, by way of apology. "She's been in shut-down, which is like being dead except you can wake up."

"Like a coma?"

"I guess so. She's stopped on some planet somewhere to rest. She sounds really weak."

"You think she'll make it back here?"

"No problem! She'll be all right. But she has to report home before she can come back."

"You know, Andrew," Kerry said quietly, lowering his voice as they neared the school and its crowding kids, "your mom's right. This is definitely spooky."

"Not when you get used to it. It doesn't feel strange at all to me now."

Caneesh watched, through three of Planet 16A's short days and nights, until Ysdran roused herself again.

'I'm back!'

He rubbed her mind in welcome, and was shocked at what he felt. She was a hundred times stronger than before she went into shut-down, but her energy supply was still dangerously low.

'It won't take long to build up my energy reserves,' Ysdran reassured him, feeling his worry and not being strong enough yet to sense the one behind it. *'And Rougita's not far now.'*

'Not far! All we have to do is pierce this planet's pollution, cross the craziest skyway in the universe, and thread through Rougita's communication cloud.'

'I didn't think it was going to be easy!'

'I've searched my files for information on repairing the instruments.'

'Great! Why didn't I think of that?'

'There's no information. They can't be repaired.'

'That's why I didn't think of it!'

She paused. Something was wrong. This was more like communicating with the alien than the normal free-flow between Caneesh and herself. Her senses must still be confused from their shut-down.

'Also, our bet has to be decided when we leave the Seventeenth System. It'll be too dangerous for you to go on training the untrainable once we hit that traffic on Skyway 41.'

Exactly as he'd intended, Ysdran forgot her worries. 'You haven't won that holiday yet! It's going to take some time to get my energy level up!'

He hadn't meant to reassure her that much. They had to get off this planet as soon as they could – that was the rule, and right now it seemed like the best rule in the universe! 'That's cheating!' he protested, as a slime of green gas smeared itself across the front windscreen.

Ysdran wasn't listening. She'd already shut him out and was calling Andrew.

Chapter Eight

Do you want to practise some more tricks? Play with gases?'

He was so glad to have her back, how could he say no? But he wasn't going to black out again.

'I thought we were friends! Why don't you trust me?'

Bitter-sweet drops of disappointment trickled away at his brain, wearing away resistance. *'Of course I trust you! It's just...'*

'Come on, you liked playing with atoms! Nobody else on your planet can do that!'

'I really did it, didn't I? Saw atoms and molecules in the air.'

'And if you'd kept on trying,' irritation spiking through her good intentions, *'you could have collected them!'*

'In what?'

'In whatever space you want! You force all the oxygen to stay in one place, and when you've got enough, condense it into a liquid.'

'Why?'

'Why? Because there's nothing like it! Because it's so beautiful; because it makes you so powerful; why else?'

'You mean you drink it? For extra energy?'

'Drink poison? How stupid do you think I am?' Her voice thickened, as if she were thinking with a mind full of chocolate, and she explained, 'The power comes from having it.'

'Like money?'

'That's not beautiful!'

'Like gold, then.' Not that he'd ever seen more than his parents' wedding rings, and Ysdran didn't consider yellow circles worth an intergalactic thought.

'The Chief Explorer,' she boasted, 'has an oxygen moat right around her home!'

For the first time she let Andrew see a clear picture of Rougita. The Chief Explorer's home looked like an indoor sports stadium with the roof on upside-down. Shimmering purple in the red sun, the smooth, flawless walls reflected the pale-blue liquid of the surrounding moat. Small, many-legged creatures guarded the bridge and patrolled the circumference of the roof.

'What are they?'

'Cilia Planet creatures: her sentinel slaves.'

She felt Andrew's shock at the word, and quickly shut off the image. 'Soldiers, I mean; I got the thought wrong. Now, I know you're afraid of playing with air, but wouldn't you like to see how water's built?'

Either liquid molecules, being slower-moving, were easier to identify than gases, or he was still in tune from the practice a week ago. Once he'd settled down with a glass of water, it didn't take long to change his focus and tune in to the smaller-than-microscopic world of jostling, floating molecules.

But what would happen if he tried to separate those molecules into oxygen and hydrogen atoms? Ysdran hadn't asked yet, but the wanting was oozing through her thoughts like toothpaste from a cracked tube.

No. There was too much he didn't understand. What if the glass exploded like a bomb?

'It can't do any harm to play with them...'

True. He didn't have to separate them, just play. Move them around. The way no one else in the world could.

He focused himself into the water until nothing existed but the drifting molecules of hydrogen and oxygen, and began to control them. He slowed them down till they formed slushy ice and speeded them up to a jiggling, seething, boiling point.

Amazing, incredible; his heart was thumping and his ears were buzzing – and he was still in-touch enough with his own body to know that he had to stop, to lean back in his chair and rub his eyes.

'Fantastic! Now...'

'Now I'm having breakfast.'

Without warning his mind was squeezed like a Chinese burn: the kind that hurts as much as a real one, when someone claims that they're only showing you how.

'Ysdran! What are you doing?'

'This constant refuelling is a ridiculous waste of time! It'll have to be cut down.' And before he could question her, she faded away.

Andrew shook his head, trying to clear the pain. He remembered her explaining that she could store up food when she was resting. She must be frustrated at needing more now – that burn had been like a power surge; her energy was flickering as she lost control.

'Don't remind me: I was going to be nice!'

Caneesh had no intention of reminding her. Caneesh seemed to be sulking. Ysdran didn't know what the sulk was about and decided she didn't care. She knew she ought to worry about why she didn't know, and decided she didn't care about that, either. She sipped steadily at her feeder tube, and began to calm down.

'You've got to admit that it's funny – he thinks it's my refuelling that needs to be cut down!'

Nearly as funny as being marooned on a planet like l6A.

'Aren't you glad you don't have to worry about refuelling?'

Grey wisps of grief seeped out before Caneesh could control them. He wasn't strong enough to call them back... Ysdran would discover the truth... how could she regain her strength if she was worrying about him?

Ysdran shut down.

Andrew was at Kerry's. And, as usual, he was losing at video games.

"Are you sure you're in touch with real-live aliens, Shewan? You can't touch any on a video!" Andrew's last plane exploded into flames. This was starting to get boring: it just didn't seem to matter anymore.

"Do you want to see what I've been doing with Ysdran? You're not going to believe it!"

She was out of reach, but he should have enough

power stored up. Striding over to the aquarium, he began to focus.

"Don't hurt the fish!"

"Relax, Milton, turning into a shark isn't till next week!"

Screen out Kerry, he told himself, screen out the room, the tank, the fish, till there was nothing but water, molecules of water, molecules of spinning atoms. Make them spin harder, jiggle them, dance them, more and more, faster and faster, higher and higher –

Kerry's shout yanked him out from the water. Atoms blurred and were lost, and normal life and the Miltons' living room reappeared. And the aquarium...

Pressed against the sides, vainly trying to push their way through the glass, brightly-coloured fish were bubbling silent protests about the waterspout and seething water in the middle of their home.

Ysdran was awake.

Caneesh was still sulking. Any welcoming thought, any flicker of a friendly mind-rub, was so well-screened that he might as well have been in shut-down himself.

Virtuously, Ysdran began to gulp from her feeder tube.

She imagined thirty-four different flavours, but they all became as tasteless as helium. She called Andrew, but it was night on his planet. He was deeply asleep, his mind in a confused sort of dance with the Tracy alien while the giant water blobs splashed in the background. Ysdran slid quickly out without waking him. The sight of entwined antennae made her feel as sick as the cartwheels he'd done when she'd asked about it. Besides, she couldn't risk a bad session now, he was so very nearly trained. So very nearly... that she was going to do it! After all the times it had seemed Caneesh was right, that the aliens were untrainable, her discovery useless – she was going to win!

No wonder Caneesh was sulky.

She transformed the cabin into a hologram of the Chief Explorer's meeting room. Dimly-glowing Senior Explorers, shrivelling with jealousy, crowded the ceiling. In the exact centre of the room, above a pond of shimmering liquid oxygen, the Chief Explorer hovered on her Crimson Pillow. Her tiny body, condensed to a dot, was sparking with joy as she announced her heir: 'Senior Explorer Ysdran!'

Still no comment from Caneesh. No acknowledgement of how proud he'd be. Not one sarcastic snip.

If she were heir to the Pillow, she could break a

few rules. She added Caneesh to the hologram. To a hissing of applause, the Chief Explorer announced that Ysdran's Companion would from now on be known as *'The Great Thinker, Caneesh!'*

Still no answer.

She couldn't deny it any longer: Caneesh was not sulking. He was not guarding thoughts from her.

Caneesh could no longer think.

*

A slave on a container ship, slipping through the Seventeenth System well to one side of notorious l6A, reported a sudden flare of pinky-yellow light piercing the green cloud. The sophisticated eye of his master was not able to see it, and the instruments hadn't recorded anything unusual. The computer reported that nothing in this solar system could possibly produce a flare of that colour. The slave was severely punished.

And on l6A, Ysdran, tickling, prodding, zapping her Companion's mind and getting as much response as if it were one of the rocks outside her windscreen, was still glowing with fury.

*

Andrew woke up once in the night, with the

vision of his friend's white face staring, mesmerized, into the seething tank. And his nervous giggle: "Luke Williamson isn't the only one who'll have to watch out! With powers like that you could rule the world."

*

The container ship had reached port and un-loaded most of its cargo before Ysdran was calm enough to think.

Caneesh must have used more energy than she'd realized at the Black Hole... Or had he used some again later, without her noticing, as they lurched from one catastrophe to another? Especially at the end, when she'd been so tired, fumbling her way through the green gas... too tired to notice her Companion pouring his life energy into hers.

Space Junk!

But that's the way it was. When a Companion's energy was gone, so was the Companion. Only one way to reverse it.

Caneesh wouldn't expect her to do that: she was an Explorer! There wasn't anything she could do.

Anything she *would* do.

Caneesh had used his energy to save her.

– To save himself, too. It wasn't the same at all – he was nothing without her – but she could get safely home without him.

It wouldn't be much fun, though. Neither would any voyage in the future. Even the bet was pointless if she couldn't gloat over Caneesh.

But Explorers didn't make sacrifices for their Companions. It wasn't a rule, more a law of the universe: planets don't change course for their moons.

Funny, though. You could die for the Chief Explorer, who probably didn't know your name. You were expected to make any sort of sacrifice for Senior Explorers (whom no one would miss if they disappeared). And the Company, of course, saw your death simply as disobedience.

Andrew hadn't been able to understand that. He'd cared that she was alive.

– Because of the power she gave him. That was all... But he cared about his mobile black hole, and it was totally powerless, as well as useless and ridiculous. (Utterly without value; it distracted him from his training; its very existence annoyed her, and she didn't want to think about it any longer!)

Her body ballooned from side to side with the force of her argument. She felt shaky and weak. What would Caneesh think?

She'd never know if she didn't do it.

Her body quivered and shrank with disgust. She floated off her atmospheric cushion and over to Caneesh's stand. She flowed into one long sinewy tentacle and wrapped herself around her Companion until she had completely covered him. As her skin touched his, energy began to soak into him.

The whales were at Look-out Point again on Tuesday afternoon. Andrew took Max and walked down with his parents before supper. They hadn't seen the calf before, and it put on a good show for them, butting and wriggling over its mother, covering her blow hole and sliding down her tail, until finally she rolled on her back and hugged it firmly with her flippers until it calmed down.

Andrew felt as proud as if he'd staged the spectacle himself. It didn't matter how many other people had watched with him, he knew he'd always have a special link with the calf he'd seen born.

"Ysdran's crazy about them, too," he confided.

"How does Ysdran know about whales?"

"I let her watch with me. She loves finding out about Earth."

His mother's smile became brighter and more determined and completely artificial. Andrew didn't notice. He was trying to call Ysdran – he wanted her to share the calf's mischievous gambolling and the whale's mammoth love.

The tricky part in an energy transfer was knowing when to stop: as the energy flowed out, it became more and more difficult to make a decision. Ysdran decided that this wouldn't be a problem for her, her mind was too strong.

She was just conscious enough to be surprised when she fell off the perch with a *squish*.

The floor was cold and hard, and she was too weak to hover. It was a long way to her feeder tube. She should have undone the emergency hose before she started.

It was a bad mistake. Her mind wasn't strong enough to undo it now; her body wasn't strong enough to creep across to it. She was as helpless as the alien when she'd begun training him.

She wasn't going to win the bet. Though Caneesh wouldn't get to his precious moon of Uturk, either. Ironic, really. His circuits were doing test checks now, sorting themselves out; Caneesh would soon be back to normal and ready to communicate – but there wouldn't be anyone for him to communicate with.

That was when she truly understood that she was going to die. Unless she swallowed some helium, she wouldn't have enough energy to survive shut-down. And she couldn't fight the blackness any longer, all she wanted was to close her eye and disappear...

One last try for the feeder tube: the latch wavered, but the emergency hose stayed where it was.

Ysdran's light flickered and grew dim.

*

Andrew was uneasy. He'd called Ysdran several times, and all he'd got was a buzzing, like the sound of a dying fluorescent light. This time it was worse – quieter, nothing but a sinister humming in his brain.

And then, so faintly that he could barely hear it above the buzz: *'Feeder tube.'*

Her powerlessness floated through him with the thought, numbing, draining. He fought it off and forced her to keep the contact open.

'Need energy... from my feeder tube.' The words appeared like flickering lights against the enveloping dark.

'Show me; let me see through your eye.'

'Can't... Won't open.'

'Come on, try!' His own were staring wide, eyebrows disappearing up his forehead as he willed her to do it.

She was too weak to answer.

'Ysdran, OPEN YOUR EYE!' The cabin was dark. He could barely make out the controls – there was

the feeder tube, but it could never stretch so far, she was too far back. *'Can you move?'*

It was a stupid question, but it got a response.

'Undo... emergency.'

'You're closing your eye!'

She opened it again, and this time he saw the emergency hose. It had a complicated latch, obviously designed by a committee who couldn't agree what an emergency was. Working through Ysdran's eye, Andrew lifted the latch, wiggled it twice, yanked it to the left, and finally called it off the wall and over to her nearly unconscious body.

'Can't gulp.'

'Yes, you can! Do it, Ysdran, or you'll die!'
– Because he'd understood from the beginning that that was what this was all about – and he couldn't think of anything much worse than living a friend's death through her own eye.

'SWALLOW THE HELIUM!'

But shouting orders, screaming at her, didn't work this time. She simply wasn't strong enough to suck.

Willing himself deeper into Ysdran's mind, he felt the hose in her mouth, and imagined sucking through a straw. The helium bubbled uselessly over her body; she cringed from the feel of it. He pictured swallowing juice, and nothing happened at all.

"Gulping" was what she always called it. He

remembered how he used to try to drink the wind when he was little, puffing out his cheeks and gulping it down hard.

He didn't know if it was working. He tried again, and this time tasted the helium. A few more tries, and he realized he could see inside the cabin again – she'd opened her eye.

'Can do it now,' he heard. *'Leave me alone.'*

On Wednesday after school Kerry wanted him to come over, but Andrew muttered an excuse. He was hoping that Ysdran would be out of shut-down, and he wanted to know what had happened.

Caneesh was checking his circuits. Everything worked. In fact – he did another computation and checked it against his memory bank – he was now a billionth of a millisecond faster than he used to be.

Ysdran was sulking. She had never been so humiliated. It was bad enough nearly killing herself to save her Companion – but to be rescued by a primitive life form!

'This would be a lonely planet if he hadn't.'

Ysdran began to cheer up. *'It shows how well I've trained him.'*

'Not well enough to win the bet!'

'That's only fine tuning. He's proven his under-standing of a slave's first rule: loyalty to his master.'

A question mark shimmered in the air.

'Don't think at me like that! I saved you because I wanted to – it's not the same at all!'

Caneesh went back to checking his circuits. He was much too contented to argue.

Andrew could have gone to Kerry's, after all: Ysdran didn't tune in until he was getting out his homework. *'If you could save your pet's life by giving it your energy, would you?'*

'Is that what you were doing?'

'I asked first.'

'Of course I would – except that it doesn't work like that on Earth! Why, what happened to Caneesh?'

'It's not important.' Why in space had she asked him? She didn't need to make her humiliation worse by discussing it. Better to concentrate on the important issue: the Great Treasure of Rougita.

And before Andrew could wonder what, how or why, he was thrown into a mirage of darkness. He was gliding through a long, narrow tunnel, using antennae to feel his way. On and infinitely on – it was tight and claustrophobic – his heart was pounding and he thought he'd never see daylight again.

Without warning, the tunnel ended. He was precariously balanced on a ledge in a large, perfectly round cave. A weak red light filtered through an opening in the domed roof. Below him, where the floor should have been, was a dully-glowing, icy blue, bottomless pool: liquid oxygen. Andrew leaned out over it, shivering with fear and awe.

Ysdran switched off the hologram, and he understood what she wanted. He wanted it too.

Sitting cross-legged on his bed, he was quickly able to focus on the air around him and see the separate molecules dancing within it. Using all his mind, he pulled out an oxygen molecule.

'There! I've done it!'

Excitement bubbled across the light years, from Andrew to Ysdran and back again. *'Don't lose it... Keep it in front of you... Now get another one!'*

He had never worked so hard. His head felt as it were being split in half.

'It's impossible – but I can do it! I'm controlling air!'

'More!' Ysdran demanded. *'Quickly!'*

He added more; there was a pile of oxygen molecules on the palm of his hand, bouncing gaily, but staying where he willed them. He was dizzy with the effort of keeping them there.

'Now condense them!'

The words swam senselessly in his brain, an echo without meaning. Then Ysdran forced the image of the pale-blue liquid into his mind. He saw the beauty of it through her eye, felt greed crowd the atoms till they could no longer dance, closer and closer till they were so dense he could see the blueness: and, suddenly, there it was. A drop of liquid blue on his palm.

He'd done it – and Ysdran was happy. More than happy. She was triumphant, and he basked in that triumph like a sunbather in the sun. He'd never been sure, but now he knew: he was as important to her as she was to him.

'It's beautiful.' He rolled the tiny drop around in his hand.

'Beautiful,' Ysdran agreed. *'You've done well.'*

Andrew flopped back against the wall and closed his eyes. *'Phew! Am I tired!'*

'You've lost it!'

Andrew opened his eyes. The oxygen had evaporated and disappeared back into the atmosphere. His visual focus was normal again; the air was clear and invisible.

Anger like the lash of a whip slashed his mind.

Another power surge, he told himself, when he could think again. She's still not well.

But all the same, he had saved her life... *'Don't you learn about manners on Rougita? You could have said thank you!'*

Chapter Nine

What did he mean about manners?'

'Rougita has the most sophisticated set of manners and rules in the universe. Thanking must be a primitive concept.'

'Happiness is a primitive concept too, isn't it?'

Caneesh's circuits whirred. *'There's a .0000001 per cent possibility that not all primitive ideas are bad.'*

It had been a long night. Ysdran had left Andrew's brain so painful and quivery that it jolted him awake every time he dozed off. Being awake meant thinking, and there were things he didn't want to think about. Things that looked nightmarish at three o'clock in the morning, and not much better at seven.

All through breakfast he fought against the nudge of her thoughts, blocking them by talking. Chattering steadily, about anything that came into his head; anything to keep her out. His dad was studying him over his coffee cup, a curious expression on his face, but, as usual, eight o'clock arrived without warning and there was no time to worry about an overtalkative son. "Keys!" he roared from the door. "Anyone seen my wallet?"

Andrew threw; his dad caught it neatly. "No tricks? You'd better stay home – you must be sick!"

His mother paused as the door slammed. "Are you well enough for school, Andy?"

It was like a bad joke – like getting back at him for all the times he'd stayed home in grade three, perfectly healthy and scared sick of Luke Williamson. And now...

Don't even think it! he told himself. How could he compare Ysdran to a vicious bully? Ysdran was cute. She was fun. When she came back to be his pet they'd do amazing tricks and be rich and famous like Kerry's mom. She'd let him see atoms, outer space, and her planet. Places that no one on Earth had ever dreamed of.

But right now he needed some time without her. Walking down the street, he counted the cars. Not good enough; *try something harder*: lists of airplanes; First World War, because he didn't know them as well. S.E.5a – that was an English one-man fighter with a 200 horsepower Wolseley Viper engine. Sopwith Camels were British, too, named after Sir Thomas Sopwith; Andrew's airplane book said they were temperamental, which always seemed a funny word for a plane. Fokkers were German triplanes; that was what the Red Baron flew; he couldn't remember his real name... There was Kerry standing at the corner, waiting for him.

"Did you study much for that test?"

"What test?"

"You forgot the science test?"

"My mom said I should have stayed home!" He couldn't even remember what they'd been studying.

Seeing Mrs. Ellis with three stacks of paper didn't give him any clues – or cheer him up. Three pages!

"One for each topic we've covered so far: pass them back and turn them over when I tell you."

Kerry gave him a good-luck grin as he handed him the last one, but Andrew had a feeling that luck might not be enough. Skimming through the questions, he knew it wasn't. Photosynthesis. Osmosis. Chlorophyll. He had vague ideas about all of them – very vague. Something to do with plants, and green stuff.

Why couldn't it have been about airplanes? Or outer space?

'Are you ready for more training?'

Andrew nearly groaned aloud. *'Not now! This test is important!'*

'Nothing is important except training!'

'What are you: a midget Mr. Armstrong? I'll talk to you after school. Now go away!'

This time he couldn't tell himself that it was a power surge. But he shoved his fist in his mouth in time to stop the scream, and at least she left him alone when it was over. There was still plenty of time to fail science.

Not like Caroline Rogers, sitting diagonally to the right of him, her busy pen scurrying across the page. Caroline Acer, she should have been called. She'd probably faint if she ever got a B. And she was always careful that her brains didn't help anyone else, always keeping the precious answers shielded as she wrote. She'd finished the first page already and was putting it neatly out of her way on her left. Upside-down, of course.

'I could turn it over,' Andrew thought suddenly. *'That's simple, compared to what I've been doing lately! And if Ysdran hadn't made me train, I would've studied, so it's not really cheating.'*

The quickest glance, and it was done; the paper flipped over without a flutter. And luckily Caroline's writing, like all her other school work, was clear, perfect and easy to read.

Andrew began furiously scribbling. He'd filled in all the blanks up to question ten before Caroline glanced down, started in surprise, and turned the page firmly upside-down.

When she was absorbed in the essay question at the bottom of page two, Andrew flipped page one over again.

There was only time for three answers before she noticed. With a ferocious glare across the aisle at Kerry, she planted her elbow square in the middle of the upside-down paper.

Andrew finished the rest on his own. If Mrs. Ellis wondered why he'd done so much better on the first section he'd say he was interested in plants. Or that he'd started feeling sick partway through. There was no way he could be caught for cheating.

Not by anyone except his best friend, anyway. "Is this your new style?" Kerry asked afterwards. "You're too busy with your new pet to study, so you get it to help you cheat!" The traffic in the hall fell silent.

"Shut up, Milton!"

"Why? It's the truth, isn't it?"

"No! You don't understand!"

"You're right I don't understand! I don't understand what's happened to you since you found this stupid alien!"

Andrew ate lunch on his own. He didn't care. He

didn't care about anything any more. The only thing that mattered now was what Ysdran would want when he got home.

A new smeary green stripe stretched across the front windscreen of "the Bucket." Caneesh had noticed that, each day they were there, the gas stuck to the ship for a little longer before it cleared – and this was the biggest smear they'd had.

'Ysdran, I know you specialize in horrible holidays, but when are we going to leave this scenic slum?'

'I'm resting!'

'You've already rested. If you swallow any more helium you'll explode. And if anyone ever finds out that we're waiting on Planet 16A...'

'It was an emergency!'

'Was,' Caneesh agreed. *'Not is.'*

'Three more days.'

'Two.'

'They're very short days.'

'All right, three. But if you expend all your extra energy on that awful alien, this waiting will be wasted and we'll never get home!'

'I'll shut down now. And for his sake I hope he'll be more reasonable when I wake up.'

In the end Andrew didn't go straight home after school. He needed some air to clear his head; needed to wonder why his best friend was turning against him. He walked down to Look-out Point.

The cliff-top was nearly deserted today, though down in the cove a motor boat was circling the baby orca and its mother. It was overloaded with camera-armed tourists and much too close to the whales.

Rage, like a white mist inside his brain, began to build up inside him. He'd failed a test; cheated; fought with Kerry – and now selfish, ignorant people were bothering his whales. It was the final insult to a completely rotten day.

But Andrew Shewan was no longer someone who had to put up with insults and rotten days. Andrew Shewan had power. And if these people wanted a whale show, he could give them one they wouldn't forget.

It was surprising how anger helped him focus. He threw his eye, as Ysdran described it, to a spot just under the calf's belly, and almost immediately began to see the water molecules. He started to jiggle them.

All he wanted was to make the whales jump and give the tourists a scare. But this calf was as ticklish

159

as he was, and it had never had a spurt of turbulent water against its belly before. It panicked.

The passengers began to scream as the baby whale changed from something cute and interesting into a ferocious monster ramming the side of their boat. The captain revved the engine as the calf submerged and came up on the far side; the boat had just begun to move when the worried mother followed. Halfway under the boat she began to breach. As she rose, spraying water from her blow hole, the boat rocked, rolled on its side, and capsized. The tourists were thrown screaming into the water; the whale shepherded its baby away from the cove and out to sea. A trail of blood lay in the water behind them.

The sea was crowded with drifting rubbish and life jackets, with thrashing arms of floundering people, with sobs and shouts and cries for help.

'Time to go!'
'I've got another half day!'
'You've got sixteen seconds. I've been charting the changes on this poisonous planet, and it will be another three hundred years before the fog fades as much as it's doing now.'
'That's a bit long to wait,' Ysdran admitted, glan-

cing out the windscreen and flicking the JUMP
button. *'But the bet's not over yet. I've got till we
reach the shipping channel.'*

The news that night said no one had been
seriously injured; a pregnant woman and her five-
year-old son were being kept in hospital for
observation. A reporter talked to the white-faced
captain. He was still shaking and had no idea what
had happened.

The segment ended with the happy clip of the
baby whale's birth, and advice from a marine
biologist who said that boats should be careful not
to threaten whales by going too close to the calves.

The news didn't mention Andrew. It didn't
explain the truth behind the terror of the people
who'd struggled to shore or clung to the overturned
boat, waiting to be rescued. It didn't say that a
twelve-year-old boy had sat in frozen tears on the
cliff-top, while around him people scrambled down
to the sea, used mobile phones to call for help and
organized rescue boats and ambulances.

It didn't even mention the trail of blood behind
the whales, or say that Andrew knew he'd betrayed
the calf he thought was his own.

He'd walked home in a daze, drifting through the

normal world of sidewalks and streets without being part of it. He went straight to bed after the news, cold, shaking and too sick to eat, and lay awake all night.

A faint buzzing at dawn announced Ysdran. *'I've got a clear run; we can do some more training.'*

He stalled for time. *'Have you left 16A?'*

She showed him. The green fog had cleared exactly as Caneesh had predicted. The only reminder of the nightmare planet was a long, green-corroded scar across the front windscreen. If they'd stayed much longer the whole ship might have dissolved! But now they were back out in open space, pointing towards a distant, thickly-scattered band of planets: *'Rougita's solar system.'*

'What will you do when you get there?'

'File my reports, then go on holiday. Caneesh and I are spending a month on Belmor.' A holographic glimpse of ruins and deserted cities; she was trying to be nice.

'What happened to the original inhabitants?'

'They... uh... decided to leave when their atmosphere had been mined out. Now. I'll be in the main shipping lane soon, so we don't have much time to finish your training.'

Something about her explanation bothered him, but there wasn't time to think about it. He couldn't stall any longer. *'I'm not training anymore.'*

'You can't stop now!'

'I've got to stop now. I mean it this time, you can't change my mind. I did something terrible yesterday, Ysdran; something evil. I didn't know I was like that. I can't be trusted with your powers.'

She felt the force of his thoughts, and knew there was no point in arguing.

Andrew let out his breath; his muscles relaxed. It was stupid to have been so worried about telling her.

Her anger caught him like a whip, sharper and stronger even than yesterday's lash. He'd never felt pain like it. Worse than when he broke his arm. Worse than anything he could imagine.

'Ysdran!' he screamed. *'Don't do that!'*

'Then do as I say!'

'No! Why should I? What do you think I am: your slave?' And as he said it, he knew. Even before her answer reached him.

'You'll be the head slave; my personal assistant, ruling the others. That's why I had to prove what you could do before I got home.'

'A head slave? I thought you were going to come back and be my pet!'

Her shock was as strong as his. *'Me? Be a pet?'*

And her laughter had pinpricks, short sharp stabs that slashed through him.

If this was a joke, it wasn't funny. *'You can't make us all slaves. You just can't!'*

'Why not? It's simple: you've got the minerals, we've got the power.'

'That's what happened to Belmor, isn't it? They didn't decide to leave – they died when you took their atmosphere!'

'Not all of them! There's a sample of each species in the Zoo.'

Andrew's mind went as black and blank as a wiped-clean blackboard. What she was saying was too hard to believe, too hard to understand. It flowed through his body like poison.

He ran to the bathroom. He vomited everything that he'd eaten the previous day, but when he'd finished, Ysdran's words were still there.

But not Ysdran herself. Had he blocked her out, or did she have some space emergency that needed all her concentration?

'I hope so!' he thought viciously. *'I hope she never gets home!'*

He staggered back to his room and collapsed onto the bed. Max jumped up beside him, wriggled into a comfortable spot under his arm, and gazed blissfully into his eyes.

"Oh, Max! You want to make everything better,

don't you? But this might be too much for you."
Max whined and wiggled. "I should have stuck
with you, shouldn't I? No magic, no tricks, just a
nice normal dog."

Andrew rubbed his face against the black velvet
of the dog's neck. But he knew there was a limit to
how long he could go on talking to Max and
blocking out Ysdran. Sooner or later he had to
think about what she'd said.

There had been hints, if only he'd seen them.
The way she'd become more and more insistent on
his training; how right from the start everything
had to be on her terms, finding out all she could
about Earth: how everything worked, the different
species, which were the strongest, which the
smartest, how long they lived... But when he
wanted to know about Rougita, the images were
small and quick and handed out like training treats
to a good dog.

Well, he'd find out now. Everyone would. Only it
wasn't quite the same, finding out as slaves instead
of scientists.

Scientists... Was it too late to call the UFO
centre? Warn them that, any day now, Earth would
be taken over by a tiny planet from an unknown
galaxy?

Way too late. Even if he showed them his powers,
they wouldn't believe in Rougita – and Ysdran was

hardly going to help. He'd probably just end up back with Dr. Lupin. If he was going to do anything, he'd have to do it on his own.

"Andrew saves the world," he thought bitterly. "Superhero Andrew."

Somehow he didn't think he was likely to find the right kind of phone booth.

Chapter Ten

I *don't think their world has any rules at all.'*

Caneesh was shocked. *'Even the most primitive worlds have rules. Rule Number Three: "The Law is Life." How would they know what to do without rules? Rule Six Thousand and Eighty-Nine: "No class except Explorers is capable of acting on their own thought."'*

'Andrew doesn't seem to understand that. He likes doing what he thinks.'

'He's a moronic monster – he's not capable of complex thought!'

'I suppose you're right. I'd hate not to be an Explorer!'

'Rule Six Thousand and Eighty-Eight: "Satisfaction in life comes from remembering our roles. The lower classes are formed to serve and obey." They'd hate to think for themselves.' Ysdran was not completely

convinced, but Caneesh had gone back to worrying over rules: *'Maybe they have a different law.'*

'Maybe.' Ysdran hardened herself until her body formed a rectangle. *'Then he'll have to learn the true one: "The only evil is disobeying the Company."'*

Andrew's parents were in the kitchen. They'd be worried if he didn't get up soon.

He glanced in the mirror in case his hair had turned white or his face shrivelled like a worried prune. They hadn't. He looked like the same old boring Andrew, a little tired maybe, but normal.

"You feeling okay, Andrew?"

Not quite normal enough to fool his mom.

"I'll be fine," he said, which became an obvious lie when he had to run to the bathroom at the sight of his cereal.

His mother was in his room when he came out. She'd taken away his dirty clothes and was changing his pillowcase. "Looks like you get a long weekend. Back to bed!" Andrew obeyed gratefully. "Will you be all right on your own? I could say I'm sick if you need me."

His mother hated lying. This might be the last nice thing he could do for her, he thought, saying, "I just need some sleep; you go to work."

"Maybe I should take you to a doctor?"

"There's nothing a doctor could do."

"I was afraid of that. Andrew, did Ysdran have something to do with the whale attacking the boat?"

He wanted to say yes. He wanted to blame Ysdran for everything... but there was only one person to blame for the boat. "It was me."

It would have been easier if his mother hadn't been so forgiving. She thought it was all a mistake; she couldn't believe that he'd do anything so bad. So stupid! He hadn't meant anyone to get hurt – but he'd taken the chance.

"Do you want to talk about it?"

"Not right now. I'll be okay, Mom. I'll sort everything out; I just need some time."

She gave him a quick, hard hug. "Get some sleep. I'll call you at lunchtime – and if you want either of us home sooner, just phone."

Surprisingly, he did sleep, right through till the phone rang at one. "Don't worry," his mother said as she hung up, "we trust you. Everything will turn out all right."

He wished he were as confident.

They were in the Home Galaxy. Things were

171

starting to look familiar. They could expect to see traffic now, and as Ysdran cut her speed back from Hyper to Cruise a warm wiggle passed from her to Caneesh and back again.

'Aren't we lucky to live in the best galaxy in the universe?'

'On the greatest planet in the galaxy!'

'We've still got the shipping lane...'

'...I know, and the communication cloud – but we're going to make it!'

'The probability is now –'

'I still don't want to know!'

The warm wiggle encircled them both. Ysdran tried to imagine what it would have been like if she hadn't saved Caneesh. There'd have been no warm wiggle. She rubbed his mind gently. *'I'm glad I did it; it's good to be going home together.'*

Andrew got dressed and opened a can of baked beans for lunch. He turned on the television, but it was all soap operas and cartoons. He couldn't settle to read. There was nothing to do. The house was pressing in on him. He decided to go for a walk. It didn't matter if anyone saw him; on the scale of things, skipping school hardly compared to everything else he'd done.

It was a mild day; it would be hot for Rougitans. Would they want to make Earth colder? Could they do that? He didn't know how powerful they were. Would they actually come and live here, or just a few –Ysdran and her tribe, colonizing the world. Taking the minerals they wanted and leaving. Or leaving nothing but an empty shell, like Belmor.

It was too crazy to be true. He'd made it all up. His mother had been adding a strange drug to his orange juice and he'd been hallucinating. No one could change the way a ball flew, move things without touching them, rearrange the air. He had no special powers.

Mechanically, he stopped to look both ways as he crossed at Mackenzie Crescent. Max decided that he owned that street and marked the sign, dog-style.

"Great, Max. That should scare them!" He glared at the sign.

Mackenzie Cres. wobbled. Starting from the top, the pole slowly crumpled and rolled neatly down to the ground. Mac es. stuck out meaninglessly from the spiral.

So much for not having special powers.

Without looking back, Andrew ran across the street and all the way to the park. He didn't need to be arrested for vandalism on top of everything else. Although, at least until Ysdran arrived, no one would believe that a twelve-year-old boy could roll a steel pole into a ball.

Oh, great. The kindergarten had taken over his park for a nature walk. After the Mackenzie Crescent incident, he was afraid to even look at them. He stamped away to a lonely, rocky bit of hill that matched his mood.

'Are you avoiding me?'

'Go away!' his mind screamed. *'I'm not your slave yet!'*

'I don't see what you're so upset about. You'll have power over everyone else.'

'I don't want power!'

'Yes, you do. To be rich and famous – that's what you wanted. Same as I do. Now we can do it together.'

'A rich and famous slave was not exactly what I had in mind!'

She was puzzled. Her confusion tickled at the corners of his mind. *'Don't you want to be my Assistant? But you liked the training! And you like the power it gives you over others.'*

Andrew groaned. *'I know, I liked doing the tricks... and okay, I liked surprising people – getting even.'*

'So?'

'So I've been a jerk! But that's no reason to punish the whole world!'

Ysdran was quiet for a moment, letting Andrew

see through her eye as she concentrated on steering past the first ship she'd met on her way home. It was heading off to the right, probably to 32F, a mineral-rich planet in an outer solar system: a huge, lumbering ship, six hundred times bigger than her tiny capsule and a thousand times clumsier and heavier to steer.

'*Slave crew,*' she thought scornfully, and Andrew, who for that split second had been too fascinated for fear, was plunged back into the horror of his own reality.

Ysdran shut the picture off. '*Clear space ahead – time for one last bit of training.*'

'*No.*'

Her irritation jabbed at him. '*You've got to try harder to be co-operative.*'

'*No, Ysdran. I don't care what you do to me: I'm not training any more.*'

'*You have to – it's our last chance!*'

The anger that had been burning, slow and hot and heavy inside him, was like a volcano erupting. Furiously, he aimed desperate arrows of hate and rage at the small, soft target. '*I'm not going to co-operate, Ysdran. Not now, not ever! I wish I'd never met you... I wish I'd let you die!*'

Like arrows off an armoured tank, his hate bounced uselessly back. A mocking laugh pricked at his mind.

Then she struck.

The pain knocked him to the ground; he lay writhing for minutes or hours, moaning while Max whined at him anxiously. *'Don't you understand?'* his mind screamed, when it finally stopped hurting enough to think. *'I'd rather be dead than a slave!'*

– Movement. That was the only thing that could save him. Andrew dropped Max's leash and rolled down the hill.

There was a sick groan, and emptiness. Andrew stopped, opened his eyes, and saw water. He was balanced on the edge of the cliff. If he'd kept on rolling...

But he hadn't. He was still on the top, with his dog alive and real and licking his face. If he could block Ysdran for long enough he might figure out something to do. Gradually his breathing went back to normal and he stumbled to his feet. "Come on, Max – let's run!"

The dog obeyed happily. Andrew watched him, the ears flapping, long back lolloping; felt his own feet strike the pavement, his chest heave. He must have looked before crossing streets, or maybe he was lucky. He didn't know. All he knew was that suddenly it was four o'clock and he was at the Miltons' front door.

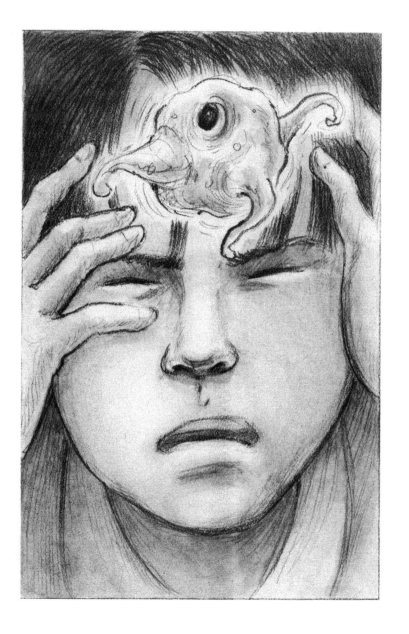

He didn't want to see anyone. And Kerry was mad at him.

Kerry had been right – not all the way, nobody could have guessed the whole thing – but more right than he was... He couldn't think about that, it was too dangerous, he had to go on blocking.

But somehow he was pressing the doorbell and Mrs. Milton was opening the door.

"I won't come in," he said. "I've got Max."

"Are you all right?" she asked. "You look flushed."

Why did everyone keep asking him that?

"I've been running." You couldn't do some real magic, could you? he wanted to beg. Strong magic to save the world?

She would have thought he was crazy. And she'd be right. Pulling flowers out of a mirror was not going to frighten –

Don't think it, he told himself.

Kerry appeared, so freckled and suspicious and ordinary that Andrew could have hugged him.

"Hi," he said instead.

Kerry's mother disappeared. Kerry still hadn't said anything.

"I've got Max," Andrew explained again, as if his friend might have suddenly gone blind. "Do you want take him for a walk?"

Kerry relaxed and bent down to the little dog, who jumped up to greet him. "Okay."

He called to his mother, and took the leash. "You sure are lucky. First thing I'll do when I leave home is get a dog."

"At least you've got all those brothers and sisters."

"Are you kidding? I'd trade them for a dog any day!"

Andrew laughed.

"Were you sick today?"

"In a way. Look, Kerry, I'm in trouble. Big trouble. But I can't talk about it."

"At home?"

"Don't ask!"

Kerry looked startled.

"Do me a favour; talk about something. Anything except that."

"Are you suggesting I'm hyper-talkative?"

Only Kerry could have come up with a word like that. And only Kerry would have put up with anything this weird. With a simple roll of his eyes, a twirl of fingers at his ears and a "Cuckoo!" to Max, he launched into his tales of the misery of life in a large family. He was halfway through the horror story of his sister Randal's ballet concert when Andrew interrupted: "What do you know about slavery?"

"Great! You'd never have to go to a ballet concert again – send a slave instead!"

"What if you were the slave?"

"I'd resign."

Andrew tried a laugh, which sounded amazingly like a sick horse. "I don't think slaves are allowed to resign."

"Come on; why the history lesson? The most we'll ever know about slavery is that story Jarred's grandfather told us about his grandfather coming up here on the Underground Railroad. It's a long way back from us, isn't it?"

"But," Andrew persisted unhappily, "what do you think it'd be like to be a slave?"

"If you were Jamie's it'd be awful; Randal's would be terrible, and if you were Chris' you'd be better off dead."

Andrew jumped. The words were so close to what he'd said to Ysdran.

"Well, what do you think? I don't suppose they'd have had the Civil War and the Railroad and everything if people liked it."

"There were slaves in Rome, too, weren't there?"

"They had fun: getting fed to the lions! Which is also what my mom's going to turn into if I don't get home in time for dinner."

That night Andrew was too tired to stop himself from thinking about it.

He wished he were smarter. Knew more about space, and what to do in terrible emergencies, and how to save the world... from someone he'd thought was a friend! Nothing could make this better, but that definitely made it worse.

He remembered a university student who'd come to talk to their class last year. Rick. An everyday, ordinary name for someone whose story was so extraordinary that part of Andrew still refused to believe it.

Rick was from Vietnam, and his mildly accented English was the only clue that this was a true story. He and his family had been boat people, escaping from their own country. "We had a good trip," he'd said softly. "We starved for three days, but the pirates didn't get us, and nobody died. And in the end we got freedom!"

His voice had lifted on the word and cracked; Andrew had looked away, embarrassed for anyone exposing their feelings like that. Freedom wasn't something you thought about when you had it. And he'd never tried to imagine living somewhere without it.

He was thinking about it now.

'The traffic's getting heavier.'
'It's not bad. Don't forget, I'm the Explorer who navigated blind through a comet ring and a meteor storm; I can easily pass a few ships!'

'*The bet finishes when we reach the shipping lane. Remember what the Great Thinker said about spinning slaves...*'

'*The Great Thinker should remember that I always do what I think! Because I've got a surprise for that spinning slave.*'

Defiantly, Andrew stood on his head for eight minutes the next morning. He wasn't as proud of it as he used to be, but at least Ysdran couldn't talk to him.

'*Yes, I can!*'

'*You don't feel sick?*'

'*I've adjusted my stabilizers for thought motion as well as space motion.*'

'*Wonderful.*'

'*I think so. Now... Oh, Space Junk!*'

She'd drifted slightly off-course and wandered into an orbiting dump of outdated and unwanted pieces of space ships.

'*When I thought "Space Junk!",*' she explained, '*I meant space junk!*'

She disappeared. So had his last possible defence. Not that he'd ever thought he could save the world by standing on his head. It was just a shame he couldn't think of anything else.

"Come on," he said to Max. "I'll take you for a walk... while there's still time."

There were a few little kids at the park again, but he was too miserable to worry about them. Making a wide detour around the spot where he'd first seen Ysdran, he took Max in a scramble down the rocks and across to his tree, where they could sit and look out over the straits and wait for Ysdran. After arguing with himself for so long, he was almost relieved to confront her – here, near the place where it had all begun.

He sat there numbly, trying to empty his mind and brace himself for her demands and the anger that would follow. He loved this place. The whole thing: the sea and the rocks and even the scruffy bit of bush they called a park, and the town beyond it. But he especially loved where he was right now, not behind his tree, but perched precariously beside it, gazing down at the choppy, blue-green waves.

'You keep thinking it's the end of your world,' she objected. *'We're going to improve – not destroy.'*

Andrew felt so completely, utterly exhausted that his mind could barely form a reply. *'It's the same thing.'*

'I don't understand.'

'So how can you take over something you don't understand?'

'Make me,' she challenged. *'Make me understand.'*

Suddenly his exhaustion was gone. He felt quick and sharp. He felt like a character in a gangster movie, gambling everything he had. *'Winner take all?'*

It was such a pat phrase – something he would never say – that he couldn't visualize it for her. *'If I explain it so that you can understand, then you have to give up.'*

'And if you can't explain?'

'Then you win. I can't stop you.'

'That's not good enough. If I win, you'll be my personal slave. You'll finish your training and then co-operate fully with the InterGalactic Mineral Exploration Company to control your planet's species and gather its wealth.'

Andrew Shewan, age twelve, gambling for the world?

'Okay.'

He'd got the world into this. If he lost he had to pay the price.

He sat for a moment, trying to gather his thoughts, staring without seeing anything, lifting Max onto his lap and smoothing his head automatically when the dog began to whine. But he couldn't think of anything to present.

The kids in the park above were getting noisier. Andrew felt old enough to be their great-grand-father. "Play," he wanted to tell them. "Play while you can." He thought of Kerry and his bickering with his brothers and sisters, and knew how much they all loved each other. He thought of Rick the university student, and Jarred's grandfather, who still had that link with tyranny. He thought of his own parents and grandparents, and his Oma who had lived through two world wars, and he looked at the sea and wondered if there would ever again be time for swimming and climbing and walking through the woods. He thought of everything except what he needed to explain to Ysdran.

'Did you mean what you thought before?' she interrupted suddenly. *'That you'd rather be dead – should have let me die?'*

Hard questions to answer honestly. How could anyone know what they'd be brave enough to do? If it were only for himself, he thought that, in the end, he'd always choose life and its ray of hope. But this wasn't just him... and as for Ysdran...

She'd been more than a friend; she'd shared his thoughts; she knew him better than any person in the world. He could barely imagine what life had been like before he met her; it would be unbearably empty without her. Even now that he hated her... how could he have watched her die?

'I meant them both. What you're doing is so wrong – so evil that I'd do anything to prevent it, no matter how hard it would be for me.'

185

'Is that a Rule?' (A flicker of triumph from Caneesh: he *knew* this world had its own primitive law!)

'It's my choice.'

Ysdran was silent again. Andrew tried to make brave-sounding statements about freedom and knew that none of them made a lot of sense. He kept getting too muddled with thinking about the people he knew being so unhappy. And the animals: he remembered Belmor, and was afraid to ask what would happen to them. The oceans would disappear once the oxygen was taken out of them; he could have cried for the baby whale who wouldn't have time to grow up.

Ysdran suddenly opened her eye to his mind and let him see through her windscreen. Straight ahead, a rapidly revolving red planet shone through a fog.

'Caneesh thinks that, now that you've seen it, you'll understand why it's the greatest planet in the universe, and you'll be proud to serve the InterGalactic Mineral Exploration Company.'

Andrew, who was not in the mood to enjoy his unique insight into space, felt as proud as a squashed bug.

'I thought he might be wrong. I think you feel the same way about your world as we do about ours – in your own primitive way, of course!'

186

Opening up still further, she showed him the interior of Starquest. Caneesh, still looking exactly like the head and shoulders of a mechanical mouse, was humming with joy.

'I owe him a holiday,' Ysdran explained. *'A month on the moon of Uturk. Funny, isn't it? I'd won that bet till I made the one with you.'*

Andrew felt like crying at the word "bet". *'Give me a bit more time,"* he pleaded.

'We don't have any more time. It's over... though in some ways I beat myself, since it was my brilliant intelligence that sorted out your shockingly muddled arguments. Still, a bet is a bet.'

'What do you mean?'

'How many ways do I have to think it? You've won, I've lost; you've got the world, I've got a spaceship with no instrument panel. Does that satisfy you?'

'Yes,' Andrew admitted honestly. Incredulously.

'The only good thing,' she added, *'is that I don't think I'd have liked sitting around being a Senior Explorer. I'll be a Junior for a long time now. So we can communicate next time I'm out.'*

'But no tricks,' Andrew told her firmly, smothering the sneaky bit of him that regretted losing his powers.

'I'm in the shipping lane! Can't transmit...'
– And she was gone. Truly gone. She might contact

him again; she might change her mind. He didn't think she would like remembering a defeat...

But he'd won. He couldn't believe it! He wanted to laugh and scream and shout and jump. He scrambled back up the path, hugging Max so tightly that the dog squeaked.

The kids in the park were still playing; he couldn't have been gone as long as it felt. A frisbee soared over his head and off the cliff, on a long straight flight out to sea.

The other kids crowded around the one who'd thrown it. "You're supposed to make it curve!"

"I did!" the boy insisted, ignoring the obvious truth.

"He did, too!" Andrew laughed, pointing for the last time, way out, over the bluff and over the sea, willing the frisbee back to his hand. "Here, catch!"

They stared at Andrew as the kid caught it and asked, "How did you *do* that?"

"Easy," said Andrew. "I'm a superhero."

5-6-7